AF576520

SMOKE STREET

PREVIOUS BOOKS BY MARK SMITH

Doctor Blues

The Delphinium Girl

The Moon Lamp

The Death of the Detective

The Middleman

Toyland

SMOKE STREET

BY MARK SMITH

William Morrow and Company, Inc. • New York • 1984

Grateful acknowledgment is made
for permission to reprint the following:

On page 96, lines from the song
"Love (Your Spell Is Everywhere),"
words by Elsie Janis, music by Edmund Goulding.

Library of Congress Cataloging in Publication Data

Smith, Mark, 1935-
Smoke street.

I. Title.
PS3569.M53766S6 1984 813'.54 84-4674
ISBN 0-688-00480-6

Printed in the United States of America

First Edition

1 2 3 4 5 6 7 8 9 10

BOOK DESIGN BY LINEY LI

SMOKE STREET

WHEN the young sailor awoke, he could do no more than stare blankly into the nighttime of his empty cabin. Only moments earlier, the captain of the *Evergreen* had paid him another of his silent visits and, after placing his ear above the sailor's mouth to better hear his words and catch the rhythm of his breathing, had gone out, shaking his head. In the wheelhouse he had remarked to his first mate, So many dreams, and this same Sally—or someone like her—in every one of them.

The ship was still at anchor, and the two men stared out across the placid harbor to the low skyline of the distant city that also served as the capital of this small Latin-American republic.

He must believe she has the strength and sympathy to save him, the mate replied at last. Or maybe it is not so much the girl herself that generates this power as it is the intense concern he feels for her. Whichever it is, the feeling must be one few men have known. Or have survived. May we all confront our Sallys at such an hour, eh, *mon capitan*?

The profundity and rightness of these remarks, along with their sensitivity, surprised the captain and moved him deeply.

To the young sailor, the visits of the captain were no more than the dimmest recollections in the darkness of his cabin, of a gold stripe flashing against the forearm of a white sleeve and of a cloud of whiskey in the air above his head. The porthole beside his bunk was open, and the reflection from the evening sky, oddly orange-tinted, shone across his sheet. He could feel the ship beneath him lift and settle, could hear the water lap against the hull and seagulls cry from across the harbor. There was also a creaking, as though a hammock, bearing weight, were swinging just beyond the bulkhead upon which he idly tapped a message with his bandaged hand.

Later, footsteps would sound above him on the deck. He could catch a voice. He would know that voice. It was that of the wheelsman who played cribbage after sundown in the galley with the second cook. Look at the rummy, the wheelsman said, finally come aboard.

Now the second set of footsteps and a watchman speaking. He was a Floridian, the young sailor would recall, who claimed to have wrestled alligators in his youth. You see me in charge of my faculties, the watchman said. You find me keen and steady. I wouldn't be alive if it were otherwise. It's a sobering country, that one. You may look the world over, and you will not find its equal for impulsiveness and cruelty. I've been cursed and chased; my life has been threatened. I had to fight my way back to the ship. Along the way I was given a taste of insurrection in the streets. Tear gas, fixed bayonets, a few potshots from the rooftops, *Viva la revolución!*—you were with me on the trip to Panama, you know the sort of horseplay. I had to persuade some native to row me out. He pulled the oars while I stood in the stern with my revolver pointed at his head. I was scared to death that when we reached this mooring, I would find the *Evergreen* had sailed for home without me.

And so you should have found her, the wheelsman said, having been yourself ashore when the captain gave the order to raise the anchor. Only an injury to one of the deckhands has kept us in the harbor. Poor devil, he was stowing the anchor chain when he was dragged, somehow, into the locker. He must have caught a limb in a chain link, trying to retrieve his hook. The winchman didn't hear the cries to slacken up. They said the chain was wound around him like a boa constrictor. They had to cut him free with torches.

Caramba! the watchman said, and gasped as

though his own body had just been broken. Dead then?

Not so lucky, the wheelsman said, but fading fast. He is below in his bunk, taking leave of everything asea and ashore.

Not young McQuade, was it? the watchman wondered.

Him or another like him.

I had nothing against McQuade, the watchman said. Nor against any of those like him.

Nor should any man, the wheelsman countered.

And my good luck is another man's misfortune, the watchman muttered.

That would appear to be how these things are balanced, replied the other.

They were pacing the deck, the two men, the pair of footsteps, side by side.

The watchman said, They haven't taken him ashore?

He won't easily return to where he wasn't wanted, the wheelsman said.

And who could blame him? the watchman said. You would be driven mad, left behind with all those sleepy, shifty *hombres* and those slinky cuties with the cotton blouses off their slender shoulders. They all carry knives and knockout drops. The place gives me the creeps. It's all voodoo and the stench of tyranny.

The footsteps came to a stop. The men were leaning over the rail, smoking their pipes in the dark. The smoke, heavier than the air itself on such a torrid night, floated downward and, like the orange light, drifted through the open porthole.

Still, bad as it was, the watchman confessed, I fell in love there all the same.

Come on, the wheelsman said.

Lost my heart completely.

Tell me about it, the wheelsman said.

The watchman sighed. Must you mock me? he said.

You're no young pup, the wheelsman chided.

Again the watchman sighed. Take a peek at her picture, he said. A real beauty, what do you think?

Quite the *señora.*

Señorita, the watchman corrected.

If you say so, said the wheelsman, scoffing.

A long silence took hold, bespeaking solitude and contemplation. Finally the wheelsman said, It's no good sleeping. It's a living hell below. Topside isn't much better. A deckhand could trade places with a stoker. The captain could run the firehole.

Look at that bloody sky, the watchman said. Ever see such an orange sky? How do they expect a man to tell sundown from dawn? We might as well be on freshwater for all the tides go in and out.

The wheelsman agreed. He said, This far south the sun doesn't ever seem to set.

And such a sun, the watchman said. It looks like a tangerine. And a banana in place of the moon. And both in the same sky together.

I can't wait until I'm in the wheelhouse on the

midnight watch, the wheelsman said, and I can set the course for Newfoundland.

The watchman said, I can't remember when I last saw a peninsula of pointed firs.

Already it's as if the wheel is spinning in my hands, the wheelsman said, and the compass points are glowing at me in the dark.

North, northeast, the watchman mumbled. I know the terminology. And steady as she goes.

The wheelsman said, When we hit the seas up north, we will wrap the sailor up inside Old Glory and slip him over the side. For a while he will sail with the currents. Dolphins will dive over him; icebergs will knock him about. Then he will do as he must do, and go down to feed the sharks.

The watchman waxed philosophical, puffing on his pipe. A man is fish food, after all, he said.

The smoke continued to descend and serpentine through the porthole, conspiring to make a face in the air above the bunk, observable in the influx of orange light.

The wheelsman said, I wonder if I ever ate a fish that ate a man?

Food for thought, the watchman said.

McQuade, meanwhile—or the sailor like him—had his own notions of where he was and what he was up to. Any talk he overheard between wheelsman and watchman was nothing but fantasy, a bad dream inspired by fever, heatstroke, too much booze. As far as he was concerned, he was still ashore, with his feet planted firmly on the earth. Hadn't he just heard with his own ears the report of the fellow with the big mustaches standing next to him of another border incident that morning? Or more likely it had occurred yesterday morning, the man explained, and the news had taken a full day to reach the capital. An occurrence at a rope bridge strung across some muddy stream or deep jungle chasm in the remote mountains of the frontier. An exchange of insults and gunfire between barefoot and sombreroed auxiliaries armed with their grandfathers' rifles, with the few victims of this scattered musketfire further mutilated by machetes. Anyway, this was how it was reported to McQuade in the sultry café where, glassy-eyed and looking neither left nor right, he again raised his glass of beer. He also picked up this piece of news: the confusing civil war that had long raged in the countryside was about to spill over in the suburbs of the city. Besides these, he heard the usual rumors. A destroyer, commandeered by its mutinous cadets and flying one of the rebel flags, had anchored itself at the mouth of the river, bottling up the heavy traffic at the docks. Or this one: a pair of cruisers from a neighboring state was steaming up the coast with orders to shell the harbor. In the afternoon an unmarked fighter plane had flown low over the city and dropped a single bomb on the presidential palace. The café had emptied with the sound of it, but McQuade had stood his ground at the bar. What does one expect in a banana republic? he said to himself. And he laughed out loud. Later, when he had himself stumbled out into the street, blinking in the tropical sunlight, he had heard the sirens and smelled the smoke.

By nightfall, McQuade had begun to regret his actions of the day. He had promised himself that on this shore leave it would be different; this time he would keep his nose clean. He would go off on his own and sample the local seafood at the typical native restaurant; would buy a map of the city and study the Spanish-American architecture that fronted on the quaint streets; would take a cab into the countryside and sightsee at the famous ancient Indian ruins the government was reclaiming from the rain forest. But what had he done instead? Why, he had acted like some kid from a prairie state the first time he stuck his foot abroad. He had stood the bar to drinks, making certain to flash his roll, and had tried to dance with b-girls, smacking his lips against their puffy faces. Drunk and separated from his shipmates, he had fallen into the company of assorted lower-class locals who took him from dive to den. Men in panamas, zebra-striped jackets and high-heeled boots. They led him down the neon-lit back alleys with their massage parlors and opium dens where sullen, girlish-looking boys and little men like skeletons whispered from the lamplit doorways, Hey, you, sailor. What you want? Girl? Dope? Magazines? Brassieres? In one of the doorways McQuade was certain he recognized the chief engineer of the *Evergreen* in the big man who stumbled out into the alley in his undershirt and shorts, and carrying his uniform in his arms. McQuade must have laughed—may even have used his index finger to make the sign of "shame on you." Because when the man saw McQuade, he said, You young kids with your whole life ahead of you, what do you know about obsessions and urges and the lonely life of a big ugly man who has to spend his nights aboard a ship at sea?

In some cabaret beneath the street, McQuade listened to a torch singer accompanied by a black man at the piano and another on the drums. The place was like a *bodega,* with wooden wine casks along the walls. The singer wore a strapless gown and sang with her shoulders squared. McQuade's waiter said she was La Flamme, an American singer who had worked her way down the coast. She winked at McQuade from the spotlit circle of her little stage. While he sprawled across the small table, spilling his party's drinks, she sang, as though to him alone:

> Love, your magic spell is everywhere
> Love, I knew you and I found you fair
> Then you left me and I laughed at fate
> Now I ask is it too late?

Later, in the course of his carousing, his companions set upon him in an alleyway, rolled him of his money and knocked him on the head. He awoke briefly to the bells of livestock being driven in the middle of the night across the city. The heat was horrible; the sweat lay on his forehead as thick as Vaseline. His back was against a wall and his useless legs were in the way of any bicycles or donkeys that might approach him through the dark.

When he next came to his senses, he heard the

rapping of automatic rifles and the shouting of a voice that sounded like that of a frightened sergeant giving orders to his young conscripts for the first time under fire.

The third time he awoke to silence. So much silence that it may have startled him in his sleep and thereafter kept him awake, alert and apprehensive. The curfew would explain the emptiness and silence. He had been warned about the curfew. It was enforced by the little soldiers in the soup-bowl helmets and leather boots, their tight-fitting uniforms a brownish-purple that recalled the color of a cowbird. He had seen them throughout the day at intersections and sentry posts, or as they clambered out the back of trucks. They all had the mustaches of adolescents and would have fought as bantamweights in the prize ring. After curfew they were said to shoot on sight. Even if they took the trouble to arrest you, count on it, you would not be seen again.

Probably the Australian sailor saved McQuade. If he was Australian. Strange if he was Australian, because McQuade was almost certain he had stood on the foredeck of the *Evergreen* and watched the sleek Australian freighter—the *Canberra* as she was called—sail out of port the day before. The sailor had come strolling down the narrow alleyway with a local girl on his arm, and the low murmur of their voices, when they paused to talk, had filled McQuade with the ache of lovesickness and romantic longing. He thought of old Mexico. A lamplit lane in the Spanish quarter; the night scent of nicotiana; almond blossoms floating through the dark; a guitar strumming in the garden beyond the crumbling wall.

Hello? Who is this? the sailor said, confronted by the body in his path. He struck a match.

So hot, *amigo,* McQuade replied.

It's the climate as much as the inner fire, said the girl.

Can't find your way back to the ship, is that the problem, mate? the sailor asked.

McQuade would have said it was if he hadn't remembered at that moment the real reason for his having left his ship and come ashore. How reckless and wayward he had been! He was so far off course! He was not here to play the tourist. Nor was it time yet to return to his ship. I have to look up a friend, he said.

I know, a girl friend, the sailor said.

McQuade nodded.

If she's the local sort you seem to have prepared yourself to meet, the Aussie said, you are better off alone.

Before McQuade could utter a word in contradiction, the Aussie understood. Oh, you have been playing the fool when you should have spent the time in looking her up, he said. Then, as he went through McQuade's pockets, he whispered in his ear, So you're in love. Who is she? Do you know? A girl from home?

Yes, McQuade said. From home. All the same he wondered where that was these days. The Dakotas came to mind. But he remembered Wisconsin also.

Let's hope she is not in any danger, the sailor

said. He must have seen McQuade wince, because he squeezed his shoulder. No good worrying, he said. You'll find her, you'll get her out, if it comes to that. And you want to put an old wrong right, is that the goal?

McQuade nodded. He would have liked to tell him it was not so much a wrong as a mistake, or an error of omission.

They must have taken everything he had on him, the sailor whispered to the girl. Money, identity papers, everything.

The girl squatted beside the Australian and leaned over to better see McQuade. Those black eyes looking into his own, the flash of cheek that glistened with heat and wet, and the large flower in her hair that brushed against his forehead, sending its perfumes and loosened petals across his face. She said, Without a passport he cannot stay here.

Nor can he go elsewhere, the sailor answered. And without his harbor pass, he can't return to his ship. Pay attention to me, mate. You must leave this place, you must get off the streets. The Seafarers, that's a safe place, it can't be far from here. You take yourself there, they will look after you there. You won't forget it, will you? Seafarers. Say it for me.

Seafarers.

It's over near what they call Smoke Street, only it's not a street so much as a district. But you won't go there. Say that for me.

Smoke Street, McQuade said.

That's the way, the sailor said. Now, on your feet

and on your way. In this country after curfew only dead men are allowed to lie about the streets.

With that, the sailor and *señorita* put their arms around each other's waists and wandered off, only to disappear through some unseen portico as though through the very brick and crumble of the wall, pushing aside the heavy overhang of jasmine that grew across the gate. This followed by an outcry of fragrance, like lemon blossoms and spice married to a sudden wave of heat. McQuade could hear their feet upon the pebbled path.

This is where I live, the girl whispered. This is my house, this is my garden. I must go inside before they miss me. It is already late.

How sweet you are, the sailor said. A little kiss before you go.

There was a rustling, as though he had embraced a sheath of leaves.

Ah, lovely, the sailor said. And now another.

You are not satisfied?

On the lips this time, he said.

This one time then, she said. There, are you happy? Now, go quickly. Take the paths I pointed out to you.

Just your movement in your clothes—any movement—the way it happens in the dark, excites me so, the sailor said. Just the sound of your movement—I don't have to actually see or feel you moving—it's so excruciating, I can't tell you, it makes my head swim so.

Will you take my flower? the girl said.

Ah, when you reach back like that to unpin it from your hair, yes, just as you are now, with your arms thrown back and your fingers busy in your hair, it's enough to make me cry out with ecstasy and pain—

You like me then? she whispered.

You make me desperate.

Good night then, she said, moving up the lane.

I am forlorn, the sailor said.

Are you weeping? she asked. And her footsteps came back a little way along the path.

You haunt me, the sailor said. You will always haunt me.

Strange adventure for McQuade, who wandered the deserted streets, seeking out the Seafarers. Blocks of small shops with doors of corrugated metal drawn and locked across their windows, and side streets of small fenced villas with palmettos in the gardens. For all he knew, Smoke Street could begin around the corner.

In self-defense, he found a safe haven in wishful thinking. If he were not here but elsewhere, he would not be lost, or in such peril. Therefore he would be elsewhere. Even if it meant returning to a time and place that never was. This was how he found himself in the Dakotas, taking a shortcut across his father's fields at night; he had only to desire it to make it so. The fields had been plowed and raked and, like the dirt road he had traveled earlier, were dusty underfoot. On the road he had been able to follow the telephone poles in the treeless landscape, a line of black uprights against the orange sky. Now he had only the one lighted window of the only farmhouse in the landscape to guide him. In the farmyard he was joined by a small black dog that kept pace, shadowlike, beside his feet until he reached the lawn. Nearby, a windmill creaked, pumping water into the wooden trough.

He passed through the kitchen into the parlor and turned the key in the glass bookcase. He searched the shelves until he found his favorite issue of *National Geographic.* This he studied at the kitchen table. When he came to the article on the windjammer cruise in the South Seas, he paused with satisfaction. Polynesia and Micronesia. Colored photographs of the ship anchored in the blue waters of an island bay. And look here, the members of the expedition tanned and bearded, exploring a coral reef underwater. Also, bathing on a beach of white sand. On the next page a map of the ship's course across the southern Pacific, island-hopping. He would take the magazine with him, he decided.

As soon as he went out the screen door, he was confronted by his father on the stoop. He was wearing the white tuxedo jacket, double-breasted and pinched at the waist, that he had worn when he had played piano in the famous Palm Room of a downtown Milwaukee hotel. Earlier, he had played saxophone in the dance band of that same hotel. When they had closed down the Palm Room, he had worked outside at the hotel entrance as a doorman. His hair was wet and had been combed straight back over his head. Behind him, the prairie sky extended in an undulating sweep of orange, with the earth beneath as black as night itself. Only the orange meeting the black below. Like a flag with two stripes. With the orange on top. The black silo and windmill in silhouette against the orange sky as though they had been bent upward from the plain of dark below.

His father said, You have gone back to my beginning. Obviously that beginning happened long before your own. I'm flattered you would want to find your self in me, but you were born elsewhere, long after I left the farm. He indicated the fields and barn. He said, What do you know about slopping hogs and baling hay?

McQuade remembered a photograph taken of his father as a boy. He wore bib overalls, a flannel shirt and a straw hat. He was posed against the checkerboard that was painted on the barn wall. The sun was on his face, bleaching it, and the bright light striking his blue eyes made him appear as blind. He had a wheat stalk in his mouth; you could see the grain cluster clearly at the end of the arch.

His father said, Why go back, McQuade? A man is always followed by his own end, surely that is elemental. It is on his heels, it dogs him day and night. He has only to slow down, never mind reverse himself, and—presto!—there is his own *finito* in place of himself along the beaten track. He threw his arm around McQuade's shoulder and indicated the far-flung horizon where black encountered orange, as though to tell him that was where his future and his fortune lay. Take advantage of your youth, he said. I know I did, right up to the very last. Even stuck out here on the farm, I never lacked for a sweetheart from the town. Picture these parts on a summer's eve. A stroll along a rural road with your arm around your best girl's waist and starlight the only brightness in the landscape. Or a scamper hand in hand across a lawn after you have removed your shoes, with the grass warm in the dark beneath your feet. There is no prettier sight than a barefoot girl hiking up her skirt and, in the same hand, carrying her shoes. One of those little moments of intense sensations. A touch, a fragrance, a come-hither look, a lump in the throat, a flash in the eyes of helplessness and invitation. It is no good kissing if you are not trembling from head to toe. Think of it, all your pent-up youthful longing rubbing up against the secret knowledge of the sweeter sex. What a delirious initiation into the realms of pleasure. What explosions and fulminations. I hope you haven't missed out on these sensations, McQuade; you were deserving of that at least. For I will say this for you. You were a likable sort of youngster, you could be trusted with responsibility, you had a kind heart, you spoke up to old people, you had a tender word for the underprivileged and you looked out for the little ones. You were like honey, my son, wild but sweet.

Then McQuade's mother was there, taking her place beside his father. She wore her nurse's uniform.

White dress and shoes, and those milky stockings that made her legs seem evanescent, like ghost legs. She had a red cross on the face of her cap and wore a blue cape around her shoulders. She had been a city girl his father had met in Minneapolis or Milwaukee, the daughter of immigrants from some country that ended in -slavia or -vania or -slovakia and, like McQuade's father, had come a long way from her origins.

Mother, McQuade said, then you are here, too.

I was at the beginning of your life, she said. It's only proper I should attend the ending.

But this is still the beginning, McQuade countered. And he took her hands, which were cool and clean, into his own.

I suppose that depends on how you look at it, she said.

What your religious beliefs are, McQuade's father interpreted. Metempsychosis. Transmigration. Whether or not you believe in resurrection or reincarnation.

Don't go back to your father's beginnings, his mother said. That won't do the job. Then she changed the subject. And death is no alternative, she said. It's not the answer. Find yourself a sweetheart, someone so full of life that she gives of it to others more lackluster than herself. Your Sally Sunstrum was such an answer. Hold on to her as tightly as you can. Pretend you are children on a roller-coaster ride. That is the sensation and the desperation you should be feeling. Let her beauty and the goodness of her nature protect you from your enemies. Let her become the bedclothes you would draw over your head when you made yourself believe the famous "croucher" was outside your bedroom door. I know this is a concept rooted deep in your subconscious that you have no chance at all of understanding.

But I would like to go to sea first, McQuade said. See a bit of the world before I settle down.

He showed her the color photographs in the *National Geographic.* The glorious windjammer in full sail. The coral reefs. The naked natives, smiling. The blue water in which they bathed, as clear as air. The cookout of turtle the crew was stewing on the beach.

You used to wear a little sailor suit, his mother said, and you sailed a toy boat upon the pond.

Maybe that put the taste for travel in me, Mother, McQuade said. Something as childish as that, happening as long ago as that. He thought, I must have believed I was in the little boat and sailing to some foreign land.

You weren't afraid of being shanghaied in those days, his mother said. I should have warned you then of foreigners and strangers. Spaniards and Germans. I should have said stay away from all men who wear fezes and turbans on their heads. Or carry canes. Also, from the sort of women who hang out in the doorways of nightclubs and abandoned buildings. Who wash themselves, squatting on bidets. I would have said, Save your money, stay aboard at Vera Cruz. Don't go near Lisbon and Macao. Now it is too late for you to benefit by such advice.

If you find yourself in trouble in some foreign

port, his father said, seek help from your consulate, those people are there to serve their citizens.

To which his mother added, If you go to the embassy, be sure to look your best. And she straightened his collar.

Wear a dinner jacket, or a handsome uniform, if you can find one, his father advised. Diplomats like to receive first impressions, and nothing does this better than a distinctive set of clothes.

To which his mother appended her own piece of inexplicable advice. Make a grand entrance, she said, in the dress of the bridegroom.

But it was not at the gates of any embassy that McQuade was to find himself, but once again in the darkness of those deserted Latin-looking streets. Only now he stood before a seedy business that bore the sign:

RAMIREZ AND KOPPLEMAN, LIMITED
SEAFARERS

Seafarers; he seized upon the word. He would be safe from the little soldiers and the notorious "death squads" inside this place; the Australian sailor had said so.

In the office window was displayed the dusty model of a passenger liner from the turn of the century and a sun-faded poster, nearly as old, announcing the sailing times of ships between this port and

Hamburg and Cartagena. Elsewhere, a few common seashells were placed at random around the shelf in some halfhearted attempt at decoration.

Inside the office, a cluttered desk, a swivel chair, a typewriter, a radio, a telephone. A black-and-white tile floor and a ceiling fan that turned so slowly you could have stopped it with your hand.

A fat man in a loose-fitting safari suit greeted him from a wicker armchair, fanning himself with a cheap Hong Kong fan while taking a large handkerchief to his throat and face. McQuade thought he looked like a professor thrown out of the university, or an exiled chief of police.

A second man was at the windows, letting down the bamboo shades. Compared to the other, this fellow looked like a small-town stay-at-home. The sort who would favor string ties and tuck a yellow pencil behind his ear; he might even answer to the name of "Slim." McQuade thought he had the face of a ticket agent, or a grocer.

Neither man, it turned out, was Ramirez or Kopleman, the men who had founded the business in an earlier era and were long since dead. Anyway, this is what they told McQuade. The fat man was de Groot; the tall man at the windows was Pendleton.

To McQuade's inquiry into the nature of their business, de Groot replied that they dealt in paperwork. Or to be more precise, he explained, in communications and transactions.

But McQuade was skeptical. They are a front for some shady operation, you can be sure of that. This was what he thought of them.

And you say you took this "Seafarers" to mean Ramirez and Koppleman? Pendleton was asking him. That is odd, to say the least. I don't know why anyone should send you to Ramirez and Koppleman.

He wasn't exactly told that, de Groot corrected. He was advised by this mysterious Australian to take himself to the Seafarers. Whatever that was supposed to mean.

And you took the word to mean us? Pendleton said. Surely you are holding something back. I wonder who really sent you. I wonder what lies behind your visit.

De Groot took over the questioning at this point. What did you say was the name of your ship?

The *Evergreen,* McQuade answered.

An American crew, I suppose.

McQuade nodded. They were Americans, as far as he knew.

But sailing under what flag? de Groot wondered. They wouldn't want to show the Stars and Stripes, given the possibility of ugly feelings among the local population. What was the nation of registry, Panama or Liberia?

McQuade tried his best to describe the flag they had flown on the fantail but failed miserably in his attempt to put the stripes and colors in their proper order.

I don't recognize it, de Groot said, shaking his head.

It must belong to one of those new African republics, Pendleton suggested. Her cargo might give us a clue. What did she carry in her hold?

McQuade shook his head.

A mysterious cargo, de Groot interpreted. Munitions, more than likely, but for which side? And tell me this: why does she continue to stay in the harbor if she has already unloaded? Are the authorities detaining her? Another mystery. My guess is she is not waiting to take on an assignment of your local bananas, but American nationals if this nasty war takes a turn for the worse.

Excuse me, but how do we know you are who you say you are? Pendleton demanded. You have no papers to identify yourself. How do we know you are off the *Evergreen*?

McQuade could remember going ashore. Some of his shipmates in their white cotton middies and bell-bottoms were gathered around him at the rail, keeping him company while he waited for the return of the launch that would take him into the city. Some had been on shore leaves before him and had returned with Spanish guitars and ukuleles as souvenirs. *Muchacha* was the one word they had all learned to say. When McQuade had stepped aboard the launch, he had said to himself with pride, You are embarked on an exotic adventure. You are calling at a foreign port of call.

Bring me back a bottle of *cerveza*! a radioman called after McQuade.

You can bring me a glass of *vino*! said a steward.

And me the stockings of a *señorita*! said the ship's carpenter, himself a Mexican-American.

Everyone on deck had laughed merrily at these remarks. McQuade remembered thinking, What wonderful shipmates they are. Like the Greek sailors in the epics of old.

Just then a small private yacht flying the local flag from its fantail had floated by, sending out the sounds of cocktail chatter and rumba music. The men on deck in their blue blazers and sunglasses must have been playboys and bankers from the city. A black-haired woman was drinking through two straws from a pineapple. These people might remember seeing McQuade depart.

How do we know you are not from the other side? Pendleton continued.

What side? McQuade asked.

That's just it, what side, indeed? Let's say the opposite side from us.

And what side are you? McQuade said.

Never mind about us. Just hope it is the same side as yourself.

Just then there was a commotion in the streets, followed by several explosions. De Groot hurried to the window. What was that? he said.

Probably just some cars backfiring, Pendleton said.

More like snipers in doorways answered by the likes of armored cars, countered de Groot. It won't be long before we are brought to the brink of sandbags and tommyguns. These fiery Latins. So unstable. So violent. Once again they will be dying in the streets.

And more mob scenes in the stinking cemeteries, Pendleton prophesied. And so many of the victims, the young men and women of this republic, so-called.

I am a pragmatist when it comes to dying young

in warfare and otherwise, de Groot said. I can't see the sense in being sacrificed willy-nilly. One should always try to see it from the victim's point of view. Oh, perhaps you wouldn't mind being cut off prematurely from these many earthly pleasures if you believed that as a warrior slain in battle, you would spend eternity in some heroes' hall in heaven, like Valhalla, drinking Danish beer and molesting buxom Brunhildes.

When I was a boy, Pendleton said, the people at the church in my hometown on this little island off the coast of Maine believed that when you died you went straight to heaven. And it didn't matter whether you were young or old. And it didn't matter either how you died, naturally or violently. It was as simple as that. He added, Of course you had to accept Jesus Christ as your savior.

And what if you were too young to have made that decision? de Groot wondered.

Golly, I don't know. The other place, I guess.

I haven't accepted Jesus Christ as my savior, de Groot confessed. But I believe in Christian virtues; I believe in them with all my heart.

How can you beat them? Pendleton said.

My point exactly, you can't, said de Groot. I believe in love. I champion tenderness and compassion. I stand firm for affection. Altruism, you have often heard me say, is a man's road to salvation. I hold as a tenet of faith that a man should lose himself in the others of this world. And by that I mean not only mankind, but all the anonymous vegetables and minerals of the planet. I support the ultimate act of selflessness whereby a man lays down his life for his fellows. Dying for a river, or to save a whale, that's not to be sneezed at either.

Putting it into practice, of course, that's another matter, Pendleton observed.

And when the job is done, de Groot continued, I wouldn't hold back the weeping for the dear departed. I admire the pulling of hair. I stand on the side of laments and keening. I maintain that all fathers, mothers and sweethearts should be allowed to throw themselves in despair across the bodies of their young men as they are lowered into their graves. Don't mistake me for an advocate of gloom, however. I welcome demonstrations of joy and merriment; I look forward to all glad occasions, such as births and weddings. Such as the wedding of our young visitor here, if he should marry. By which he meant McQuade.

Better that he should marry than die young, Pendleton said.

You must go to the embassy, de Groot said. It is the only way to save yourself and, at the same time, to learn the whereabouts of your girl friend in the countryside. If she is a teacher, as you say, she would be sure to be registered with the embassy.

She must be a teacher, McQuade said. What else could she be? When I saw her last, she was a student at a teachers' college in Minnesota. And he thought: I tossed a snowball against her window, and she leaned out into the snowfall and said, Who is that throwing snowballs against my window? And I answered from the darkness, Come and see.

Strange that she should be a schoolteacher, de Groot observed. Usually the American girls who turn up along this coast are caberet singers or exotic dancers. When they grow too fatigued to sing and dance, they become the mistresses of government ministers and generals.

I don't want to alarm you, Pendleton said, but a man could stand before a map and put his finger on few places in the countryside that he could safely call secure. Your friend could be in great danger. And you could put your life at risk should you go in search of her. For example, not long ago two French schoolteachers were murdered in a mountain province outside the city. One of the women's fathers flew over to see if he could discover who was responsible for such a brutal crime. He rented a car at the airport and drove immediately into the countryside. He has not been heard from since. And who knows how many German missionaries and Scandinavian do-gooders with leftist leanings have disappeared? As an American, your friend could be mistaken for a government agent. So many American teachers over here are engaged in some low-level form of spying, which, of course, is why the government sends them.

On the other hand, de Groot was quick to add, she may have already moved into the city. At this very moment she may be safe inside the embassy, awaiting your arrival. And if she were working for the Americans in some capacity, they would be certain to bring her out at the first indication of any danger.

But McQuade thought, These men are probably spies of some sort themselves. Americans like himself, they were monitoring the deteriorating situation in the country.

The problem is how to get you safely to the embassy, de Groot said. The same identity papers you will need to obtain from the embassy in order to go in search of your girl friend in the hinterlands you will also need in traveling from Ramirez and Koppleman to the embassy, you see the bind. If you were stopped along the way and discovered to carry no papers, you would most certainly be arrested.

Again, I have no wish to alarm you, Pendleton said, but there have been hundreds of reports of indiscriminate executions. If they don't shoot you down in the street in front of strangers, they drive you out into the badlands and shoot you in a ditch. For a woman, it goes without saying, it is much worse, even though her fate comes to the same as a man's in the end. The situation is terribly confused right now. No one knows who is on what side, and no one can afford in such times to take chances. Your executioners could be government soldiers in civilian clothes, or they could be terrorists pretending to be soldiers. And in either case, no matter which side you were on, they would be willing to believe you were on the other.

But McQuade was not taking into account any danger to himself. His only fear was that Sally might be numbered among the many missing. As if to contradict this fear, he closed his eyes and cast about him for a time and place where he was certain he could find her. That was how he came to see himself in the dark of night, standing beneath the shade trees around the farmhouse. He had walked a long way to get here; he had carried his jacket over his shoulder and paused at the crossroads to take a handkerchief to his face. Such a sultry evening. He seated himself on the lawn swing, which he made go back and forth. There was piano playing inside the house. The parlor windows were lighted. He thought he saw the face of Sally on the veranda; she was at the balustrade, in a spot between the lilac bushes. Her face was moon-bright in the darkness. Just then a prairie town sent up its Fourth-of-July fireworks, and McQuade turned his attention to the colorful display against the brilliant backdrop of the orange sky.

Then Sally appeared before him on the lawn. She wore a white gown, like muslin; its edges billowed in a breeze he neither felt nor heard. She was so white, and the night around her was so black.

Is that you, Sally? he cried. Have you come home again? And in your wedding dress, poor dear.

She seemed frightened of him. She kept her distance. She twisted a lock of hair around her finger. Her gown was wet and mud-splattered; the hem was torn. She smelled like sweetbrier in the rain. And have you drowned yourself in some stream? he said. And is this your ghost I see, poor thing?

I am alive, she said. I wouldn't kill myself for you. Nor for anyone. Life goes on, McQuade. You can't take me with you.

What a thing to say! he said.

One of the nine men the "death squad" had abducted during the night resembled McQuade, except that he was smaller and older. Lately he had gone under the name of Fortune. This was a shortening of "soldier of fortune" which he had been, more or less, for a number of years. He had been both a mercenary and a vagabond, and was, depending how you looked at it, countryless or a citizen of the world. Fortune was only the most recent of many aliases. His face was weather-beaten and so nut-brown that he could almost be mistaken for a native. He looked like someone familiar with airstrips hacked out of the jungle and illuminated by the headlights of the trucks waiting to take on the secret cargoes of the small planes. Also, like one versed in the exchange of currencies. He had been brought with the others to the basement of a building where, he assumed, he would be shot.

He was interrogated in a room next to the lavatory into which the other captives had been herded. His interrogator was dressed in olive fatigues and wore a red handkerchief across his face. Even so, Fortune was certain he recognized the blue eyes in combination with the black wavy hair, like twisted wires, as belonging to the notorious Major Hilario. An army office, famous for his malice, he had been a minister in the previous junta and still had strong ties to the present government. On the damp stone wall behind the major, as though to legitimize the proceedings, was draped the flag of the secret society, a brown stripe above a green stripe and a red monkey inside a yellow circle in the center.

The major looked Fortune over. I know you, he said. I know you generically; your kind is crawling with drugs and dollars. And, specifically, you helped the old regime.

No, Fortune answered, they helped me.

The more reason you should pay us back, the major said, since you received but did not give. And he laughed at the cleverness of his response. He went on, Yes, you made your bundle. You were in the dope business at the source of the Amazon, don't deny it or I shall smash your face. You were with the Americans in Asia, for that I should shave your ears. How many times have you been in and out of Cuba? Don't answer that or I shall become incensed and cut out your guts. Well, what do you have to say for yourself?

I should like to go on living, Fortune said.

You have no mother, the major lectured, ignoring him. You are without a family. You possess no land. Your kind are parasites. You swear no allegiance. You make no commitments. You do not know the meaning of sacrifice. You are thistle seeds, you are blown in the wind, but you don't come down, the birds should eat you. You have no reason to die except to try to save yourselves. Oh, you might die for money, you mercenary, you deserve a bullet. You have no ideals. If you were an enemy on the other side, I would torture you myself before I had you drilled. But your kind aren't worthy of my hatred, I can't get worked up over such a man as you. Saying this, he returned Fortune to the large underground lavatory where he joined his fellow prisoners. These were university professors, newspaper editors and high school teachers who had been abducted from their clubs and homes. Two of them were in pajamas.

The same masked guards who delivered Fortune to his prison took out the first group of prisoners to be shot. Because Fortune had gone to his left instead of to his right, he was numbered among the second group. How had he come to such a bad end? he asked himself as he watched the unhappy men march out.

He had known he was taking a desperate gamble by entering the city. Even so, he could not believe how careless he had been! What else explained his actions except that he was deranged by love? He had made no plan, carried no false papers, had worn no disguise. He had walked openly upon the streets. Before a crowd of astonished passersby, he had been set upon by a gang of masked thugs out for an evening of rounding up their enemies or settling old scores. He had been manhandled and forced at gunpoint into a private car. No one had come to his aid or so much as cried out for help. He still did not know whether he had been fingered or merely recognized. Maybe he was simply unlucky enough to have been mistaken for someone else.

His contacts had warned him to stay out of the country entirely, never mind returning to a place as dangerous as the city. They had reported rumors of a price on his head, literally on the delivery of his decapitated head. He had come back regardless, working his way by canoe through the mosquito-infested mangrove swamps along the northern coast where he had friends among the local Negroes. Even then, when he learned firsthand of the massacres and repressions, he should have lit out for the highlands, where the Indians would have hidden him until he could have crossed the frontier to safety in the north. He might have done so if it had not been for Gabriella. He had not known how much he loved her—how much he could love anyone—until he had lost track of her. He had had to leave her behind when, warned that a secret society had sentenced him to death, he had fled for his life in the night. On his return to the country, he had learned she had been reported seen inside the capital and had sent messages to her old address. But nothing came of these attempts. The reluctance of his confederates to meet his gaze when he spoke of her made him believe that they suspected she was imprisoned, if not already dead. In his jungle hideout he had gone crazy with his helplessness and drunk whiskey straight from the bottle far into the night. He had sat in his poncho, laying out his many small black-and-white snapshots of Gabriella on the bamboo table as other men might lay out playing cards in a game of solitaire while the incessant rains leaked through the palm-leaf roof into the hut. Sometimes in his desperation he would throw his knife passionately into the walls. Finally he had been driven to come himself into the city. If he discovered that she was dead, he would gladly join her!

The paunchy man standing next to Fortune in the lavatory said he was a political-science teacher in the local high school; he assumed he had been singled out for his political opinions. Fortune could imagine the photograph of the man in tomorrow's newspapers, laid out on his back in a ditch or gutter, the flies around his bloody face and a placard with a filthy name scribbled on it pinned to his chest. He saw the same picture of himself.

The high school teacher was nudging him. Up there, do you see it? he said. He pointed to a tiny opening in the stone wall high above the sink that Fortune had not noticed before. What do you think it is? the man wondered.

A window? Fortune said.

I think so, too, the man whispered. You must try it. You are small and agile, you have a chance to escape. For me, it is like a glimpse of heaven, that little window. To see it and know you have no wings.

Try it quickly, said one of the others who had overheard them. His hands were tied behind his back and he had been beaten about the face. Live to tell our story.

The others did not encourage him. Even the two who urged him on would not look him in the face.

If you escape, the teacher said, you can go here. You will be safe here. He wrote a word down on a piece of paper, using a pen from his suit. He folded the paper and handed it to Fortune.

Wait! said another man. He wore a goatee and looked important. Both lenses of his pince-nez were shattered. He scribbled a message on a scrap of paper. His hand trembled so that he could barely write the words.

Fortune kept his eye on the distant window. Hurry, please, he said.

One of the men down the line began to whimper.

Silence, ordered the man whose hands were tied.

At last the note-writer folded his message and, after pressing it to his lips, gave it to Fortune. Tears were in his eyes. Give this to my wife, he said.

Fortune leaped onto the sink and worked his way up the wall, which was wet and slimy, taking hold of the pipes. He pulled himself up to a shelf of bricks that jutted out just below the window and to which he clung, momentarily, hand and foot, like some rock climber on a bulging face. If a guard entered, he wondered, would he see him on the wall? The men were far below, watching him. He tried the window, and it pushed out into he knew not what. Miraculously, he passed through the narrow opening, scraping his hips.

Good man, someone said below.

He exited into a rectangular chamber that may have been a drain and was probably beneath the street. A grate was overhead through which light filtered, creating a grid effect across the floor. It was too far up for him to reach. He ran his hands along the stone walls and felt nothing but the smoothness of the surface. No ladder was mortared into the sides, nor was there anything else he could step on or grasp. He tried to run up the walls, grabbing for the grate. He did not come close. He returned to the window. Below, the men were standing as before, waiting. Except that now their heads were bowed, as though in prayer. Across the room, near the urinals, he saw the broom. He crawled headfirst back through the window and perched on the brick shelf just below. He was terrified that the guards would return at just this moment. The broom, he whispered, motioning with his hand that they should send it up.

But the men didn't appear to hear him. Or if they did, they could not comprehend his desire to sweep. The man was whimpering again. The tethered man's lips moved as he prayed.

Please, the broom! he called aloud.

The high school teacher came out of his trance. He looked up and saw him. He saw the broom next. He stood on the sink and held the broom up to Fortune as far as he could raise it. He performed this task as though bidden by a mesmerist. Fortune reached down and grasped the tip of the handle in his fingers.

Good luck, the teacher said. He winked and shook his fist.

Just then Fortune heard the shouts from behind the walls.

Viva la revolución! said one voice.

Viva la democracia! cried another.

Viva el amor! screamed a third.

This followed by a ragged volley of rifle shots that echoed underground.

Fortune returned through the window and into the chamber. He pushed up on the grate with the brush of the broom, wondering what he would do if it were bolted down. The bristles bent until the metal band that bound them was flush against the grill. By this time he was standing on tiptoe, reaching up as far as his arms could stretch. He pushed, jumping. The grill gave, came up, moved off its flange. Next, he worked it around until its smaller side coincided with the longer wall. Then he hooked it with the broom handle and slid it down into the chamber until it rested on the floor. This was tricky and noisy. Just then he heard the pistol shots—the coups de grâce. The spaces in the grill were just wide enough for him to insert his fingertips and toes, and he scrambled up it as though it were a ladder.

He found himself on a deserted street—he had not realized the lavatory had been so far beneath the ground. He hurried off.

When he was a block away, he ducked behind a wall and opened the note that had the name of the safe place the teacher had written down for him. Instead, he opened the other man's note to his wife. It read:

> Dearest Rosalita, When I am dead, the last thing they will see in my eyes is a vision of your lovely face. All who look upon me will see you there and wonder at such a miracle! Think of me in the black earth of our nation, with yourself in my eyes and staring for all time into the darkness of eternal night!

The fool! The message was undeliverable. He had forgotten to give Fortune his wife's address.

Fortune opened up the right note. Seafarers, was all it said.

McQuade found himself at the American Embassy, having made it safely across the city in broad daylight without incident and with no other disguise than a large straw hat on his head. De Groot had drawn him a map, saying you are here as he tapped his pencil on the Seafarers, and the embassy is here. Now I will mark your route across the city. And he drew a line between the two x's. In this direction lies Smoke Street; go around it, he said. Don't go near it. Then he sent him down the busiest and noisiest of boulevards, jammed with the jostling crowds at the outdoor markets, motorbikes and packed buses stalled in the heavy traffic. As instructed, he entered the front gate of the embassy, where a crowd of locals was queued up in the hope of obtaining visas and was watched over by plainclothes policemen in sunglasses and a small contingent of little soldiers, rifles slung on their shoulders. He walked right past them all and presented himself boldly to the marine guard at the front door. I am an American in trouble, he said, just as he was told to say.

Go in then, the marine guard said.

In the reception hall he was met by Rice, the naval attaché. A young navy officer and Annapolis man, he wore a white uniform made colorful by braids and ribbons. He looked McQuade up and down. How do we know you haven't sold your passport? he demanded. There is a strong market for American passports. You may have heard of the stolen-passport ring in Tangier?

McQuade thought this an odd remark to make. Surely Tangier was a long way from here.

You would be surprised how many Americans

conveniently lose their passports when they are broke or down on their luck, the attaché said.

McQuade could not say he cared for the attitude this man had adopted toward him. Why are you so authoritative? he said.

The question had the desired effect. The naval attaché backed down. You are right to criticize me, he admitted. Unfortunately, we are all on edge around here. It's an internal affair. I can't say more except that we seem to have our share of unhappy mysteries. And he put his hand to his brow as though he suffered from a headache. We will contact the captain of the *Evergreen,* he said, and learn if he can verify your story.

While McQuade waited, he wandered out into the embassy garden, which abounded, oddly, in banana trees. A peculiar choice for an ornamental in that there were many plantations of them just outside of town. Perhaps some earlier ambassador had had an eccentric fondness for the plant. All the bananas in their heavy bunches were as green as the broad leaves upon which they grew.

McQuade sat down on the patio just outside the library. The French doors were open, and he couldn't help but overhear a shouting match between two men inside that room. One of them was Rice, the naval attaché. The other, he would learn, was Sanderson. The sight of you continues to infuriate me, the attaché said to Sanderson. You betray the generous hospitality of the ambassador by creating the most shocking scandal, and yet here is the poor man, forced for the sake of his daughter, whom you have betrayed, to continue to put you up as his guest. You do see the irony in the situation.

Sanderson was almost the same age as McQuade, whom he resembled, except that he was fairer, taller and better-looking. He had rather longish blond hair and a drooping mustache of the same color, and wore a white cotton suit, a bit wrinkled, which gave him the appearance of a doctor, and a red carnation in his lapel. You forget that the ambassador himself implored me to stay, he answered. In the name of friendship, I don't see how I could have refused. If I didn't have feelings of responsibility and guilt for what happened to his daughter, you would have gladly seen the last of me as soon as yesterday.

I should think you would feel responsible, said the naval attaché. And sorry, too, damned sorry. Your behavior was outrageous. You were "ungentlemanly."

Sanderson bristled at the word. Only with difficulty was he able to keep himself in check. Oh, we agree on that much, he said. But see it from my point of view. I don't care to be made a fool of in public for whatever reason.

To my mind she was the party humiliated, responded the other.

Of course, it will do no good to point out to you that the scene was of her own making, Sanderson said.

Only you and she will ever know the truth of that for certain, the other said. She was not only humilitated, she was mortified. Count yourself lucky we weren't fitted out in the ceremonial dress of the old navy with the plumed hats and swords. I swear, I would have drawn mine and come after you—I might have killed you for what you had done just then. Or maybe I should have just chased you about the dance floor, smacking you across the backside with the flat of the blade.

A fitting finale for a comic operetta! Sanderson quipped. And in the process you would have made an even bigger fool of yourself than poor Mitzi made of herself. You would have outshone even the likes of me. My dear fellow, you would have stolen the show.

By God, McQuade was impressed by this Sanderson. He thought, This fellow can hold his own. He acts superior because he is superior and knows he has the upper hand.

I don't like your coolness, said the naval attaché. I don't care for your lip. You will be held responsible if Mitzi fails to recover.

It hasn't occurred to you that she might be faking? Sanderson responded. It has occurred to me.

It occurs to me to ask you what you did for her when you were alone with her in her apartment afterward? the other asked. His voice cracked as he spoke.

Exactly what I should have done, Sanderson said. I attempted to keep her calm. I also tried to force her to face up to reality. What else took place between us is no concern of yours. I assure you, however, it was nothing very romantic.

Meaning what? the other wondered. That there was intimacy without romance? He was red-faced.

A look came across the face of Sanderson then

that seemed to ask, What is this all about? Finally he said, Why should your concern for Mitzi be so much greater than her father's?

Instead of answering, the naval attaché turned on his heels and marched away. But not before he pounded his fist into his palm. Smack! Like that. Just the once.

I think you have answered me! Sanderson called after him.

Puzzled, McQuade came and stood in the open doorway while Sanderson wandered over to the piano and picked out a tune with one finger. Then he sat down and played a chorus of "Lost in a Fog." When he was finished, he spun around on the stool and confronted McQuade standing on the threshold of the room. So they won't let you leave either, he said.

McQuade gathered from this remark that he must have overheard his own earlier conversation with the naval attaché.

It seems you and I share something of the same predicament, Sanderson continued. I want to go into the interior where the struggles and atrocities are taking place. I want to write eyewitness reports from the battlefields.

Are you with a newspaper? McQuade wondered.

Nothing so professional as that, Sanderson admitted. I'm a would-be journalist. But I want to meet the fighters and their leaders face to face and test myself under fire. Maybe a book will be the result of this adventure. Maybe if I am persuaded that right and justice belong more on one side than the other, I will see it as my duty to make its cause my own.

You mean become a guerrilla yourself? McQuade said.

If I said I believed that possible, would you think me a romantic innocent? Sanderson said.

McQuade denied that he would. He sensed an immediate camaraderie between himself and Sanderson. Now it is my turn to tell you a secret, he said. Don't tell anyone, but I'm not returning to my ship, not yet anyway, no matter what they think. I plan to head for the interior myself. I have a girl out there I want to look up.

Good for you, Sanderson said. Is she lost?

I hardly know, McQuade confessed. I certainly hope she isn't.

If she is, you will find her, Sanderson said. Count on it. Now, let me suggest that when we are free to leave the embassy we join forces and travel into the interior together.

It was just what McQuade wanted most to hear. Shake hands on it then, he said.

If we are to be pals, Sanderson said, then I must tell you what the argument just now was all about, for we should have no secrets between us.

What a strange story he told McQuade. Before coming to this country he had written to Mitzi Killanin, an old friend from both his prep school and university days, and the daughter of the American ambassador, on the chance that this connection would gain him access to the combatants and war zones of the countryside. She had sent him a telegram, inviting him to come when he pleased. It so happened that the night of his arrival coincided with a formal reception given by the embassy in honor of one of the generals who had recently joined the junta. It had been arranged that Sanderson would serve as Mitzi's escort for the evening. The guest list was made up of admirals, professors, the old landowning aristocracy, government ministers and the local diplomatic corps. Tails and ties, satin sashes with sunburst decorations and almost everyone in sunglasses. And Mitzi herself, dressed like a homecoming queen in low-cut chiffon gown, white gloves up to the elbows and a tiara atop her honey-colored hair. She and Sanderson had waltzed together. Then they danced the rumba and also some local dance, very popular, that was reminiscent of "La Cucaracha." Worn out, Sanderson had retired to the fountain in the inner courtyard into which he was observed to dip his hand. He also liked the sound of the water splash and, when he leaned over, the tingle of the spray upon his face. Close at hand was a punchbowl he used to keep his cup full.

With the dancing over, the ambassador and the government officials made the usual exchange of toasts. This accomplished, the ambassador tapped his spoon against his wineglass and called for attention. His daughter, Mitzi, wished to make an important announcement. Mitzi came forward to polite applause and announced her engagement to Mr. Tyler Sanderson, Esquire, her escort for the evening. She pointed him out as though inviting him to join her up front, or at least to identify himself by a wave of hand. Outbursts of applause, cries of congratulations. What a delightful surprise! the ambassador exclaimed. And utterly unexpected! I had almost given up living to see this day. I marvel how you young people were able to keep it such a secret!

He was not the only one surprised, Sanderson said. That was the first I heard of my engagement. The attaché is right, I behaved badly. I was overtired from my travels, I had drunk too many tonics to ease my fever, I had spent too much time at the punchbowl when, suddenly, on all sides of me was this crush of dignitaries and their matronly wives pumping my hand and making me clink champagne glasses. And Mitzi wouldn't shut up about our engagement; she went on and on about how long we had known each other, how strongly we felt about each other, how romantically we behaved together, what our lives would be like after we married. She even addressed questions to me, such as, Where was it that we first met, Tyler, I bet you don't remember? I kept interrupting her from the floor. This is a joke, I said, loudly enough for all to hear. I don't know why this announcement has been made, but I can assure you that not a word of it is true. Pretty soon I was as good as shouting. We are not engaged! I insisted. And never will be! I caught sight of the naval attaché glaring at me as though he could kill me, he was right about that much.

But why did she say so if you weren't engaged? McQuade wondered. There must have been some misunderstanding.

Not on my part, McQuade. I assure you, I gave her no such understanding. I knew she had liked me once, that she had had a powerful attraction for me, but I believed her feelings belonged to the past.

You didn't seduce her? McQuade asked.

What a word, and from a sailor, too, Sanderson said. Does anyone use it these days?

How wonderful to be loved as desperately as this Mitzi loved Sanderson! That was what McQuade thought.

Eventually I got the better of our shouting match, Sanderson explained, and Mitzi broke down and cried in front of everyone. She had to cover her face with her hands. How clearly I saw her fingers, and I actually remember remarking on the flashing of her rings. Fortunately I had sense enough to lead her away. Which brings us to the real mystery of this bewildering affair. She had been in perfect health when I put her to bed, but the next morning when I tried to look in on her, I was informed she was still sleeping; and, in the evening, after having my inquiries ignored all that afternoon, I was told she appeared to have lapsed into a coma. At first I suspected she must have taken drugs—the naval attaché went so far as to accuse me of administering an overdose. But the doctor dismissed such a possibility. All she has done these past two days is to sleep in her bed. Or pretend to sleep. Her eyes are shut tight and not so much as a muscle of her body can be seen to move. And that is where we are today.

What a mysterious story you have told, McQuade exclaimed. It defies a simple explanation.

* * *

Just then the ambassador came into the library and greeted them. He was a small dapper man who favored his old school tie and black-watch slacks. She still sleeps, he announced, and refuses to awaken. The doctor says there is no need to remove her to a hospital, not that I would permit it in any case. But let the doctor tell you so himself. And he introduced the doctor, who had accompanied him into the room, a local man and professor at the medical university.

It is as the ambassador has said, the doctor reported. It is as though time has stopped for the patient while it continues for the rest of us.

A suspended state, the ambassador said.

That would be my diagnosis, the doctor said. Nothing at all is wrong with her so far as I can ascertain. No sign of injury, no symptom of disease. Her pulse beat and temperature are nearly normal. Her sleeping is a great mystery, unexplained perhaps by science. It is as though she has been placed under a spell. One almost suspects voodoo. It is my opinion, however, that she is either genuinely lovesick or that she has willed herself into a sleep from which she does not choose to awaken.

And if either is the case, the ambassador said, your presence here, Sanderson, can only be a blessing. You must continue to stay on until this is settled one way or another. On the other hand, if the doctor is mistaken and she has been struck down with a serious illness that confounds the medical profession, you are hardly to blame for that coincidence. Whatever ails her, you may be sure we will get to the bottom of it when she comes to again.

McQuade said to himself, He is certainly putting the best possible face on an unhappy situation.

As soon as the doctor made his exit, the ambassador said, But why should we take the doctor's word? Let us look in on Mitzi and judge for ourselves, the doctor says we can't disturb. He opened his arms and invited McQuade, also, to come along.

Upstairs, the ambassador opened the double doors of his daughter's bedroom simultaneously in a grand gesture, allowing them to gaze in on his daughter, where she lay motionless beneath the satiny turned-down covers of her bed. McQuade, startled, wondered if she might be dead.

Mitzi, the father called out. Here are friends come to see you.

There was no response from her bed.

The ambassador went to her bedside and lifted her hand. Please open your eyes, your dear eyes, he pleaded. Neither her eyelids nor her mouth moved, and her hand, when her father let it fall, dropped lifelessly to the bed. It's so pathetic, he said. You can shake her by the shoulders, shout in her ear, nothing moves her. If it is an act of will, it is a powerful performance.

McQuade was astonished by the beauty of the girl. Her hair was arranged stylishly on the pillow around her face, which was made up as though she had been posed for a fashion photographer. Her negligee was open at the throat, and McQuade fixed his gaze upon the small breast shapes beneath the cloth for the gentle signs of her breathing. Negligee, bedclothes, hair, all shone equally with that same silken luminosity and softness that reminded McQuade of lingerie. He found himself thinking, If Sanderson doesn't want her, perhaps I can have her.

Have you seen enough? the ambassador inquired. And when both McQuade and Sanderson nodded that they had, he closed the double doors. As they strolled down the hall, he separated McQuade from Sanderson and linked McQuade's arm into his own. What explains it, McQuade? he said. Too many private schools and special privileges, perhaps too many summers spent sailing in pleasant waters. Maybe she has lived too cloistered a life inside the embassy to have had close friends and lovers. Perhaps the few men she has encountered have been so intimidated by her beauty, fortune and position that they haven't dared to approach her, never mind make serious advances or profess their undying love. In her loneliness she may have become high-strung, hysterical; she may have gone so far as to convince herself that she was unloved except in her fantasy life, where she was beset by admirers. Perhaps it came about that she was no longer able to separate fantasy from reality.

Meaning she believed it when she announced she was engaged to Sanderson? McQuade said.

Ah, so you see it that way, too? the ambassador said. It's always good to have a fresh opinion. Saying this, he wandered off.

Alone, McQuade turned his thoughts to Mitzi. What if he had met her before he had made his promises to Sally? She might have been his other half, which, the philosopher says, all men seek, explaining the attraction between the sexes. He saw himself sharing in her active life. The pair of them on horseback galloping through a Vermont meadow, jumping a stockade fence, fording a mountain stream. Or beaching a small sailboat on the shore of a West Indian island. McQuade in white ducks rolled up to the knees, a pirate sash for a belt, a wide-brimmed straw hat, a cheroot clenched between his teeth. He waded in the turquoise water while Mitzi made herself comfortable on the golden sand of the beach. These images, and others, excited him, and he experienced an irrepressible urge to sneak back to her room and lie down beside her on the bed. He was certain he could do it without disturbing her. He would turn his head on his pillow so that he faced her and could watch the many subtleties of her face in sleep.

But when he returned to her room, he saw that Sanderson had gotten there before him. He had drawn a chair up close to Mitzi on the bed. His back was to McQuade, who, masking his disappointment, quickly shut the doors.

Ah, Mitzi, Sanderson said, leaning forward in his chair, can't you hear me? Sure, you can. You can't help it. Is it as your father says about you? If so, why me, old chum? Did you set your mind to punish me for not loving you as I might have done these many years? Is it the old story of a woman scorned? Now you won't so much as talk to me. Nor to anyone else.

Come now, behave yourself, do this for your own sake. Don't give up on life. Think of all the good times we had together. The time we skiied the White Mountains and sailed off Castine—they were worth repeating, wouldn't you say? Believe me, times like those will come again. Why give up so much as a few days of your life for someone as unworthy as myself? You know me, Mitzi, you must have seen through me for years—how could you have failed to see the truth? They call me good-looking, the fair-haired boy, the lucky one. But I'm missing something, Mitzi. Some hardness or brightness in the heart or soul. I have yet to make a mark—have yet to do any good, to be, in any way, a factor. What makes you desire such a man as me? Why be drawn to incompleteness and failure? Show some sense, old chum. Don't be unreasonable. And he kissed her gently on the lips. Then placed his cheek against her own. If it's a choice between guilt and death, he whispered, choose guilt. You can choose it any number of times. Death you choose only once. He rose and selected a mirror from the dresser. With hands trembling, he held it only inches above her face. When he was satisfied that its glass was cloudy with her breath, he replaced it noiselessly.

Unknown to Sanderson, he had been observed by the naval attaché, who had replaced McQuade in the doorway. So you don't love her after all, he said.

Not so as to admit we are engaged, Sanderson replied.

The attaché looked furious.

But you love her, don't you? Sanderson said. I understand that now, I should have guessed as much.

I am beside myself, the naval attaché said.

Did you have an understanding?

I thought we did.

You were lovers then?

You may say so; you wouldn't hear me say it.

Then this must be as great a shock to you as it is to me, Sanderson said. And harder to bear, certainly.

There was never any indication that you were in the picture, the attaché said, until your letter arrived and she could talk of nothing but your visit. Oh, she had mentioned you before, I knew you had been classmates. There was your skiing trip to New Hampshire, and then out to Utah. And the football weekend at Chapel Hill. But I didn't pay attention to this kind of talk. I was envious, of course.

I don't understand why I should have been in her thoughts, Sanderson said, shaking his head.

You must stay by her side, the attaché advised, and do what you can.

I have said that I would.

Then we must shake hands, said the naval attaché, and try to be friends.

Downstairs, Captain Lundholm of the *Evergreen*, in the company of the ambassador, awaited McQuade. Good old Captain Lundholm. His was that world of whiskey inhabited by yellow-haired and redheaded men. He claimed he had been ashore on business, staying at the local hotel where the embassy had contacted him. The truth was, he had been on a binge, and his white uniform looked as though it was the first suit of clothes he had worn in days. I have told them who you say you are, McQuade, he announced. As soon as they make out your new papers, you had best return to the ship. If the situation hereabouts gets any worse, we may leave port on short notice. The immigration people can make it difficult if we don't depart with all our crew. In other words, who comes in here must go out. You wouldn't want to hold us up, I'm sure. I know you would not want to put your ship in danger. On the other hand, you wouldn't want us to sail away and leave you stranded.

Come now, you show the situation in the worst possible light, the ambassador complained. Things have quieted down considerably in recent days. There are only a few reports of sporadic fighting in the countryside.

Maybe that means all hell is about to break loose, the captain said. You know, the proverbial calm before the storm.

It is my experience, the ambassador said, that all these stories of civil war and insurrection are greatly exaggerated by the present government for its own political reasons. It helps them to stay in power by securing economic and military aid from our own government. Which, I am sorry to say, is only too willing to help them fight their war.

You would know best, of course, the captain said.

I would go where you please, the ambassador advised McQuade, subject to a little common sense. The generals assure me that the city and its environs are completely secure. And vast stretches of the countryside have never known such peace.

The captain took McQuade aside. He smelled of whiskey. I should be careful all the same, he cautioned. I wouldn't necessarily trust the opinion of such an optimist as our ambassador—to hell with him. It will be safer aboard the ship than anywhere hereabouts. And especially when we are under way and steaming northward through the open seas.

The naval attaché was looking for McQuade. We have news of your friend, Sally Sunstrum, he announced. Good news. We know she is a schoolteacher in a small village in a mountain province. It is a pacified village, loyal to the government, in a secure area. We have had no reports of trouble there. And guess what? The village, although remote and in the highlands, is no more than fifteen miles from the capital, only that far from where you stand. Think of it, as close as that to you.

And safe, you say?

I guarantee it.

And I can see her?

Thanks to your captain, you have your new papers. You may go where you please.

McQuade had to sit down and rest a spell, he was so overjoyed at the news. He would see Sally before another day was out.

Meanwhile, the ambassador, with his hands behind his back, had wandered to the window. Take a look at that orange sky, he said. Never have I seen such a sky before.

The captain joined him there. He said, Let an old

salt tell you that you don't often encounter a hue of that orange in the sky this late in the season. You only get something like it in the Straits of Malay. And along the coast of Zanzibar. Maybe in the open sea along Sri Lanka, which they used to call Ceylon. But those tints are a far cry from the intensity of this.

McQuade made sure to get Sanderson alone. I am leaving to find Sally, he said. Come with me. We will never have a better chance to penetrate the interior.

To McQuade's surprise, Sanderson was reluctant to go. I gave my word to stay here as long as I was needed, he said. That should not prevent you, however, from going to your friend as quickly as you can.

What is this I am hearing? McQuade said. Is this an adventurous reporter speaking? How can you pass up such a chance to explore the countryside? You may not get another. I promise you, we will only be gone for a day, two days at most. Then you will be back at Mitzi's bedside. You know her condition can't be taken seriously, you have said as much yourself. Happily, he observed that his argument was having the desired effect.

If I did leave for a day or two, Sanderson conceded, I suppose that would show her how I really feel about her, how thoughtless and irresponsible I really am. It could make her face the truth at last.

That's the way to talk, McQuade said.

Sanderson told the marine guard at the gate that he and McQuade were off for a hike in the foothills outside the city, which explained the small packs they had strapped to their backs. As soon as they were out of sight of the embassy, they broke into a run, laughing like boys who had escaped from school. But McQuade was soon winded and limping, and they hired an ancient taxi to drive them to the outskirts of the city, where they learned at the café where the buses stopped, that it was not known when the next bus would be leaving for the mountains and Sally's village. Sanderson had an idea. They would rent horses from the stable across the street.

Sanderson was an expert horseman, but McQuade was a novice in the saddle.

Watch me, Sanderson said, as he mounted. Do as I do.

Yippee! McQuade hollered, feeling the horse beneath his thighs.

Both men stuck large straw sombreros on their heads and tied handkerchiefs around their necks. They opened their shirts to their navels and rode with the reins in one hand and the other resting on a hip. They found their way by consulting the small cloth map the naval attaché had given them and by learning the directions from the natives they met along the route. They had not gone far before they encountered a field hand eating his dinner in a ditch beside the road who claimed to know of the village to which they were headed, although he himself had never been there. He thought his father had visited the village, though. He had also heard about the beautiful "Americana" who lived in it. She was like a saint to the people, teaching them to read and write and healing their sicknesses.

As they continued their climb up the rocky roads and trails, steep in places, they passed almond orchards and coffee plantations, and could make out, in the distance, misty waterfalls pouring threadlike through the hanging jungle. They encountered neither soldiers nor guerrillas along the way. Not even a local policeman. McQuade could not imagine a more peaceful countryside than this.

To help pass the time, Sanderson insisted upon explaining the complicated political situation to McQuade. The country was ruled by a junta, a centralist military government that had replaced a series of more repressive regimes. This junta was supported to some degree by several right-wing private armies and societies, secret for the most part, and financed by the wealthy old families and large landowners, and said to include members of the army and government itself. The notorious "death squads" were alleged to come from these groups. Although they waged war against the reformist elements of the government, their terrorist tactics were concentrated mainly on the Marxist guerrillas who, until recently, had kept to the countryside. The guerrillas were identifiable by their jungle fatigues, which set them apart from an older revolutionary group, an agrarian and populist movement whose members wore straw hats and sombreros, although it was rumored that these two forces had recently become allied. In addition, there were the Negroes in the swamps near the coast and the Indians in the jungle interior, each led by their local leaders, demanding some form of equality and autonomy. So you see how the government is caught in the middle, Sanderson said.

I don't want to hear any more of this, McQuade said. What does it have to do with us? The war is a long way from here. And it gets farther with every step we take. And kicking his heels into his horse's ribs like an experienced rider and flicking the reins from side to side against its flanks, he hurried on ahead.

Men on donkeys acknowledged them, their saddlebags full of stones; workers in the fields waved at them; women with wicker baskets of vegetables on their arms gazed down at the ground in their shyness and barefoot children came out of their adobes to stare at them as they passed; small barking dogs ran alongside their horses.

On the advice of a shepherd, they left the washed-out road and took a shortcut on a trail across a meadow. When they came out of a ravine, the village that was their destination came into view. White adobe houses perched on the rocky rise above. On the outskirts of the place, they were met by a delegation of villagers.

The naval attaché must have wired ahead with the news of our arrival, Sanderson said. It is the only explanation.

A trio of elders held their hats before them in their hands and made speeches of welcome, bowing. Young women hung garlands of camellias around the horses' necks and asked for the visitors' sombreros so that they might stuff the bands with flowers. Young men took their horses by the bridle and led them, surrounded by the enlarging crowd, into the center of the village.

On the second-story veranda of the small Spanish hotel on the square, Sally herself awaited McQuade. She stood alone before the rustic grillwork of the railing. She had dressed herself in a simple low-cut peasant blouse, colorfully embroidered with birds and flowers, and a full skirt, also embroidered, with a bouquet of red-and-white flowers in her arms. When McQuade came into view, she stood on her tiptoes and waved.

McQuade came off his horse in a daze. A barefoot boy was on hand to take the reins. For a moment, McQuade stood in the bright sunlight, brushing the dust from his clothes, gazing up at Sally with the wonder of his simple happiness. Behind him, the musicians appeared. Guitars, strummed loudly on the bass strings, were joined by the pipes of Pan and a goatskin drum. McQuade threw out his arms and bounded up the steps. Sally was in his arms at last. How soft and warm she was, as though he had found her sleeping on a sunlit lawn. She smelled like apple blossoms and laundered bedsheets that had dried in the sun. He kissed her on the eyes and mouth, tasting her salt, for her face was as wet as his own. Why, it was as if they had had their first lovers' quarrel—such a minor episode—and they were making up, kissing away each other's tears. He called her his honey, his dear, his beautiful bride-to-be, told her that in her arms he would always be safe, that she was his haven in this storm of life, that he wasn't one of those unlucky fellows who had to cast about high and low for his darling, having through no virtue of his own fallen upon her first thing. And then, having been so thoughtless as to lose her, had been granted the good fortune to find her again. And he kissed her bare shoulders, which were brown and warm, pressing his lips to her bones.

In the square below, the musicians with the guitars and mandolins were singing,

> The whole village is asleep
> the clock strikes midnight
> a boy walks across the field
> searching for the house of his girl friend.

It moved McQuade to tears, he cried so easily these days. He sat down on the bench that ran the length of the veranda and put his head in his arms, and his arms on the rail. For a long time he was inconsolable.

So here you are, he said to Sally when he had recovered, like a flower in the sunshine just after the shower.

And here you are, she answered, like a bee in the flower.

The heavy wooden door to her rustic bedroom off the veranda stood open. The white linen sheets upon the bed, the rush-covered floor, the whitewashed walls. And on the primitive table, a vase of flowers, a bottle of wine, a bowl of milk covered with a napkin, a dozen eggs.

* * *

A feast was held in McQuade's honor in the village park beside the hotel. The area had been swept clear, and the brush marks of the brooms were still visible in the gravel. Long tables had been put out beneath the trees, and had been set with tortillas and succotash and melons in several shapes and sizes. McQuade and Sally were seated at the head of the longest table. During the feast, they were serenaded by the guitar players and the singing of the village women, and were surrounded by smiling barefoot children.

I can see how much these people love you, McQuade said to Sally. How much you have given of yourself to them. That is how one should behave, isn't it, devoting oneself to others? Look at the glow it has brought to your own face. And it is the children you love best, that is easy to see. Never have I beheld such tenderness. He was full of gratitude for these demonstrations of her goodness. Overcome, he took his napkin to his face.

Sanderson, who sat at his right, showed that he was touched by this outpouring of emotion. Compose yourself, old chum, he said.

McQuade was overcome a second time, this time by sudden feelings of affection for his friend. What more can a man ask than the love of a woman who is his one and only, and the special friendship of one man? he said. Sally is my love, and you, Sanderson, are my friend, and I have you both at once, and in the same place, too; what a lucky man I am!

In the village square outside the park, the boys had begun a game of soccer.

McQuade and Sally rose from the table and made their way through the company, which parted to let them pass. Men held up shot glasses and bottles of liquor in salute, inviting everyone to drink their health. Long life! they shouted. They teased them, too. Tell us, young ones, they said, where are you going? And for what reason?

McQuade said, To a secret place, friends. And it is a secret path that takes us there. And what we do there has been done before, and will be done again. He wanted only to go into the cornfield below, where he could collect himself and be alone with Sally.

When the villagers saw what they were up to, they laughed and called out, Will you be honeymooning with your sweetheart?

McQuade blushed. So did Sally, at his side.

The musicians grouped up behind them and tried to follow them into the corn. But the women came to the edge of the field and called them back, saying, Shame on you! Don't be nosy! Come back where you are wanted and sing to us!

When they were alone in the corn rows, McQuade took Sally by the hands and said, The first time I saw you, you were combing out your hair beside the lake where you were swimming, and I approached you and asked your name before I kissed you. Dear heart, from that beginning, who would have guessed it would have come to this?

I did, she said. I knew how it would end from the beginning.

Love at first sight, Sally, he said. But it doesn't end here. This is just the beginning.

We were in a public garden once, she said. It was in Wisconsin somewhere. We walked a grassy path between the flower borders. One border was all phlox, all colors and in bloom. The other border was all verbena.

And suddenly I turned to you and kissed you, McQuade said, completing the story.

Impulsively! she said.

And you answered me, he said.

Eagerly!

Forgive me, McQuade said, but I never knew until this moment that that was the very best moment of my life.

I will always love you, McQuade, she said. Just as much at the end as at the beginning.

Later, McQuade found himself alone in the field. Sally had turned back and rejoined the feast. His head was swimming with the wine. The only sound in the landscape was the rattle of the castanets coming from the village. Or was it only the cries of the insects? In a distant field, a band of field workers in the usual straw hats and smocks walked along a stone wall, carrying rakes and shovels on their shoulders. A herd of pigs trotted alongside them like hounds returning from a hunt. Men from the next village, probably, McQuade said to himself. In the opposite direction he made out a herd of horses galloping riderless in a cloud of dust. Wild horses, he surmised. He walked down into a little pasture. He was curious because a woman was down there, just where the pasture was divided by a stream. She stood alone there. She was a vision of his mother. As before, in her nurse's uniform.

I recall my own wedding night, she said. I was showing your father how to dance the polka at our wedding party when a guest snuck up and stole my shoe. He held it up for ransom while I limped about the dance floor. This was a custom from the Old Country, where your maternal grandparents were born. Your father and his ushers, they were native Americans, they didn't know they were responsible for protecting the bride's trousseau. They had to pay a ransom of a hundred dollars to retrieve my shoe. Naturally, this money was turned over to the bride.

She took her son in her arms. Watch out for mischief-makers around your own bride, she warned. Don't be caught napping, or with your defenses down. The ransom they will ask of you, my son, will be your life.

Come now, Mother, McQuade said, surely not my life.

That much and no more, his mother said.

McQuade returned up the pathway to the park, where he found only silence and empty tables. At the hotel, the door to Sally's room was closed. She must be resting where it is cool, he thought. He would not disturb her peace. It was siesta time; that explained the shuttered houses and deserted streets. As he wandered through the narrow lanes and alleys, neither a soul nor a shadow could be seen. Flies buzzed in the sunlight about his face; they covered the mouth of a dog sleeping in the gutter. In the village square he came across Sanderson sitting alone in what little shade he could find beneath the awning of a deserted shop.

I have discovered an important piece of news in your absence, Sanderson said. The villagers have told me that Sally is a great favorite of Christiano, the local guerrilla chief. He protects her, and favors this village. She taught him how to read and write.

McQuade could not fathom why his friend passed on this information so reluctantly, almost as if it were bad news. Wonderful! McQuade answered. No wonder this place is so peaceful, he guarantees her safety.

You see it in that happy light? Sanderson said.

I see it in the best of lights, McQuade answered. The more certain we are of Sally's security, the easier it is for us to leave. Come, show me where you put the horses. We should get away quickly, before the siesta is over and the village comes alive again.

But you have only just arrived, Sanderson said, incredulous. Why must you leave?

So that I can return, McQuade answered. And the sooner I leave, the sooner I return. Surely the logic of this requires no explanation.

Nevertheless, explain yourself, Sanderson said.

In the capital I will make the necessary arrangements for the *Evergreen* to leave without me,

McQuade said. And if the good captain refuses my request, then I will try to persuade him to wait for me as long as he can.

What will you do when you return to the village? Sanderson asked.

Stay here with Sally, or take her away with me, whichever seems best.

Extend your present visit, Sanderson pleaded. Don't run off like this.

You would stay here without me? McQuade demanded.

Would it surprise you if I confessed the thought has crossed my mind? Sanderson said.

Must I remind you then of your own promise to return to Mitzi? McQuade said. And how her life may be held in the balance?

Sanderson hung his head. If you are right in reminding me, he said, then why am I so full of misgivings?

As I am myself, McQuade conceded. Nevertheless, my mind is made up. I am determined to go.

Then you must say good-bye to Sally and the others, Sanderson advised. And explain our reasons for going back.

McQuade said, If we told these villagers of our plans to leave, they would make us undergo a week of feasting. Such are the laws of hospitality among such simple folk.

But McQuade had another reason for wanting to be elsewhere. Dwelling in this perfect place was like watching a brilliant sunset. The sight was so extravagant that one felt crushed and had to avert the eyes.

One was unworthy of such a vision. Come quickly, if you are my friend, McQuade said.

But in the stables where their horses had been quartered they found empty stalls instead of horses.

The villagers must have borrowed them, was Sanderson's suggestion.

Why, then, we shall borrow theirs, McQuade replied.

But no horses were to be found anywhere in the stables. Nor could they find so much as a pony in the village. Nor a living person at such a noonday hour except for an old man in the village square, but he could not explain the absence of so many horses.

Horsethieves, became McQuade's explanation for the mystery. Without horses, he didn't know what to do.

Just then a double-decker bus overloaded with country people, vegetables and chickens came lurching from a side street into the square, backfiring and smoking, with clouds of feathers floating out the windows. The driver stuck his head out of the cab and, shouting above the rattle of the ancient motor, asked the old man the name of the village. When the old man informed him at some length of his location, the driver said, Then we have missed the fork for sure, we never stop at such a town! Those bandits have changed the signs again!

No, you made the wrong turn! the passengers complained. We said so at the time, but you were too proud to listen to poor people!

This renewed an old argument, and the driver stood up on his seat and exchanged insults with his passengers. In the course of his defense, he mentioned "bandits" again and drew his finger like a knife across his throat. He wore a green hat sideways on his head, with the visor over one ear.

The old villager gave him directions to find the road to the capital, drawing lines with a stick in the gritty sand of the square.

He is headed for the capital! McQuade exclaimed. What a piece of luck! And he hopped on the wooden running board and pulled Sanderson up after him as the bus jerked away. They found seats behind the driver between two large Indian women with caged cockerels and rabbits on their laps.

They had no sooner left the village behind them than McQuade said to Sanderson, Why is it, my friend, that whenever I leave a place or person I have this sense of something left unsaid or undone?

They swayed and bounced their way through the mountain country in a heavy mist before re-emerging in the sunlight. On the many curves, the driver leaned on his horn, ordering goats and carts out of his path. On downhill grades, the bus raced out of control, the driver complaining of the brakes. On the steeper inclines, the passengers had to disembark and push from behind. Cheerfully, McQuade rolled up his sleeves, calling for the others to give him a hand. Then the bus broke down, and the driver lay in the shade between the tires, patching up the undercarriage with his wrenches while the passengers sat in the hot sun, mopping their faces.

During the breakdown, they were overtaken by a small convoy of army trucks, driven at a breakneck speed. A woman was seated between the soldiers in one of the cabs. McQuade caught a blurry glimpse of her as they passed.

Some of the passengers had first to push the bus to get its motor started and then to chase after it, huffing and waving their arms, until they could be hauled on board by the many hands reaching out for them through the doors and windows. They went only a short way before the bus was stopped at a roadblock set up by government troops. They ordered the driver outside, where they conversed with him in the road. Then they waved the bus on its way.

That village where you came from, the bus driver said over his shoulder to Sanderson and McQuade as they drove on, the government soldiers say a battalion of their comrades attacked it not so long after we left the place. First they had a spy drive off all the horses so that the villagers could not escape. The soldiers must have been hiding in the fields outside the village when you were there. They were hoping to trap the famous Christiano.

Turn around or let us out, either one, McQuade ordered. We must go back!

Hold on, the driver said, catching McQuade by the shirt and pulling him back from the running board before he could leap into the road. The soldiers were driven out by a strong counterattack from the guerrillas. The soldiers escaped with the American schoolteacher who lived there as their prisoner. They passed this way not long ago.

McQuade remembered the woman in the truck. It had been Sally!

She is no longer behind us, the driver said, but ahead of us. By now she has reached the city.

Step on it then! said McQuade.

When they reached the lowlands, the bus was stopped by a group of guerrillas in jungle fatigues who stood in the road. Some carried automatic weapons and wore cartridge belts crisscrossing their chests. They ordered everyone off the bus so that they could search it. They were surprised to discover two Americans aboard and separated them from the others.

Your driver says you are friends of the American schoolteacher, the officer in charge said. She was a great favorite of Christiano, the local leader of our forces.

He was in love with her, a soldier said. We have just learned the sad news that he was killed trying to rescue her.

She is an American, the officer said. That may carry some weight with the soldiers. On the other hand, who knows what they will do to her because of her friendship with Christiano?

They will do terrible things, predicted the soldier.

We must get to the city, McQuade said.

One moment, the officer said. Who are you two, anyway? What makes you think you are our friends? Or the other way around? Whose side are you on, anyway? What are you doing so far out in the country? It may take a long time to learn the answers to such questions. Perhaps you have forgotten how your country has supported this government and supplied its army with the weapons and advisers it has used against us in the field.

He nodded to one of the soldiers who, in turn, motioned at McQuade and Sanderson with the barrel of his rifle. Then he marched them off into the orchard beside the road. The ground was bare and dusty beneath the trees, not a blade of grass or a weed showing.

They plan to shoot us, is there any doubt of that? Sanderson whispered.

I don't care what happens to me now, McQuade answered.

When they were a hundred yards into the orchard, and in plain view of the bus and guerrillas gathered in the road, their guard motioned for them to squat on a spot of ground between the trees. He lit a cigarette. With his hand cupped around the ash, he pointed to the city that stretched below them. Until then, McQuade had not realized they were close enough to see the city. It was like a vast sprawl of adobe villages interrupted by a few skyscrapers and squares of green that were parks of palm trees, with the blue sea of the harbor just beyond. Puffs of smoke rose up at scattered locations between the buildings, and even at this distance, they could feel the delayed concussions of the shells. It was strange how the sky was empty, though; not a plane flew overhead.

The rebel forces are trying to take the city, Sanderson said in disbelief. The long-awaited offensive has begun.

What do we do now? McQuade wondered.

Suddenly a commotion back in the road. Shouting and several shots, and the soldiers and passengers seeking cover behind the bus. On the heights across the way, a patrol of armed men was making its way down a streambed. Now the guerrilla leader and two of his soldiers were standing in the road, waving their rifles and yelling at the advancing patrol. Apparently the newcomers were not government irregulars, but other guerrillas who had just now mistakenly fired on their own.

Wait here, you two, said the soldier guarding them. He returned to the road, but he was in no hurry.

Run for it, Sanderson said. And stay low. They dashed down the hillside, in and out of trees, kicking up the dirt.

To reach the city, they had first to wade the wide but shallow river on the outskirts, then thread their way through the suburbs of squatters' shacks that Sanderson explained were a rebel stronghold. The noise of the raging battle became louder as they ran. They were running toward the worst of it, McQuade pointed out, instead of away from it, but what choice did they have?

At this rate we will never make it as far as the embassy, Sanderson said. Look at the smoke pouring up from that quarter of the city!

I know of a safe place, said McQuade. It must be close by.

At the Seafarers, McQuade and Sanderson found the bamboo blinds drawn upon the office windows and, in the gloom inside, what resembled a council of war around a small table on which was set a burning candle and a bottle of the local whiskey. Besides de Groot and Pendleton, there were two strangers, a man and a woman.

So you have made it a second time, de Groot said to McQuade in greeting. You must meet a man even luckier than yourself. And he introduced McQuade to the man he called Fortune. A small, dark, balding man who looked both exhausted and exultant, as though he had just been rescued after months of wandering forlornly in the jungle. The sort of man, McQuade decided, who would not hesitate to pull a gun on you.

You see before you, de Groot explained, a man who has escaped his own execution. Strange that someone should have given him our business name as a place of refuge. It was the same with yourself, McQuade.

When I had no hope left for love or life, Fortune said, miraculously I was granted both, and almost in the same breath. Not only am I alive when I have no right to be, but I have found Gabriella.

Gabriella sat beside him. She was petite and olive-skinned, and must have been some admixture of Spanish, Indian and Negro. McQuade predicted she would possess a dark history, and that she was initiated into the practice of secret vices, pleasurable to extremes. Already she drove him to a fever pitch of helpless infatuation. He felt compelled to take her dark hands, which were as perfect and as haunting as her face, into his own; if only he could press his lips against those slender fingers. He was afraid she knew exactly the nature of the eroticism he was feeling. From such a woman, a man could have no secrets. How easy it would be to leave you after a night of ecstasy, her eyes alone said as much. McQuade read heartbreak in her face—it was his own. McQuade noticed that Sanderson was staring at her, his face frightened and unbelieving. And that she returned his helpless gaze. Returned it tenfold, as though to mock him, until at last, sighing and putting his hands to his head as though he were confounded or in pain, he turned away.

How can you explain it? Fortune asked as he reached for the whiskey. First, I escape the firing squad. Next, I run down the streets in search of Gabriella at her last known address, the same to which I sent my messages that went unanswered, and which is the only lead I have, and who should answer my knock but Gabriella! Not in her early grave or in the hands of the soldiers, as I had imagined so often in my despair when I was hiding in the country, but safe and sound in her own place all along. I found her exactly where I could not find her. How can you explain such a mystery?

Who would have thought you would have searched for me in the same place you received no answer? Gabriella said. The search was not worth endangering your life.

It was worth more, Fortune said in his own defense, and I would have given more, if I had had more to give. He turned his attention to consoling McQuade. How ironic that you should lose your girl at the very moment I have been fortunate enough to find mine, he said. We must do everything we can to rescue your friend. Take advantage of me while I am in such a helpful mood, so unlike me, too, as Gabriella can attest. All my life I have looked out for myself and managed nicely on my own. Every man for himself, that was my battlecry. Now I want to reach out beyond myself, I want to share my luck, repay what I have been given, I don't know how to say it. But saving my life today and finding Gabriella, it was like discovering that life itself could become the best of daydreams. As though it actually had become that dream. As though I had died but was granted a second life to live. I am already dead, think of it like that. Tell yourselves that the man you see before you is something extra, a bonus, a ghost. If I am killed the next time, how can I lose, having already won? I have already been granted so much more than I deserve. So much more than has been given you and you and you. And he went around the table, pointing. Forgive me, he continued, I am not an intellectual, I am no philosopher. But life and death are not each other's opposites. His eyes became cloudy. He placed his arm around Gabriella and drew her close. There is only love and death with nothing in between. Life without love is worse than death, it is not worth anything. I tell you, if you are not in your lover's arms, you might as well be hanging from a lamppost.

Where you were once melancholy, Gabriella said, you are now morbid—too much for your own good. Or for mine. We must escape from this city, we must leave this country, quickly. Her eyes were on Sanderson as she spoke, as though she communicated with the two men equally, one with her words and the other with her eyes. For himself, McQuade would have chosen the eyes.

We will do as you say, of course, Fortune acknowledged. And these men will help us to escape. But first we must help them save the girl. I have already worked out a plan. McQuade has said the soldiers brought his Sally to the city as a prisoner. That means they have probably detained her at the central army barracks. If so, it should be easy to free her, since I have connections there. Unfortunately, I don't have the money we need to bribe the guards. He turned to Sanderson and said, Unlike your friend, you give every appearance of possessing money—and old money, too, would be my guess.

I would have to send for it, Sanderson said, if we are speaking of a large sum.

Can you lay hands on it at the embassy? Fortune said. You must have connections there.

He is a friend of the ambassador and his daughter, McQuade explained.

See if you can borrow what we need from them, Fortune advised. Dollars if you get them. But gold or jewelry would do as well.

I will do what I can, Sanderson promised.

Unfortunately, the streets are much too dangerous for him to travel on, Gabriella said.

Perhaps not so dangerous, Fortune said. Haven't you noticed how the gunfire has died down? Listen!

He was right. Except for a few random shots, the streets were quiet.

A lull in the battle, Fortune said. What did I tell you? Luck is with us.

Pendleton had been listening to the radio, a receiver held against his ear. He said, A cease-fire has been declared, they have just broadcast the news. It is to last for two hours.

Time enough for Sanderson to do his work, Fortune predicted. And for the rest of us to do our own.

What do you say, Sanderson, are you going? McQuade said. You wanted to experience adventures of this sort firsthand. You had a taste of it in the countryside; now you have another opportunity to face up to danger in the streets. You will have an exciting story to write down and send back to the people in the States.

Sanderson said, I will do what I can.

Are you frightened? McQuade wondered.

Scared to death, Sanderson said.

As bad as when they held us captive in the orchard?

Sanderson said, Worse, I think.

Fortune took Sanderson out the back way, intending to show him the streets he should take.

This gave McQuade the chance to speak to Gabriella alone. Who is Fortune? he asked. What do you know about his life in the States?

Two facts only, she answered. He was born in Idaho, and he spent time, as a young man, in a prison in Colorado.

Why is his life in danger now?

She shrugged. Perhaps he had too many connections with the old regime, she suggested. Or maybe there is a powerful syndicate in this part of the world that believes he has reneged on a deal.

And we can trust him?

More than you should trust yourself, she said.

I don't understand how he failed to find you all those times, McQuade said. By your own admission, you were where he sought you all along.

Then you have guessed the secret, haven't you? she said.

Yes! McQuade admitted.

So for you there is no mystery. I was there to receive his messages, and I did receive them. But I ignored them. I even told his messengers to tell him his efforts were futile, I could not be found.

McQuade scratched his head.

Poor McQuade, she said. You were clever enough to see how, but you don't see why this should be so. And yet the answer to this is as obvious as the other, it is the only answer.

McQuade responded by putting his cheek against the back of her hand.

McQuade settled back and listened in on the pensive conversation Pendleton and de Groot were having.

Pendleton said, I suppose just about every little town and hamlet across the globe has its Smoke Street.

Do you honestly believe that Smoke is as common as Main and Elm? de Groot inquired.

Smoke Street

There was a Smoke Street on the island where I spent my childhood, Pendleton continued. But it didn't stretch far enough to reach the village in the harbor. You may say it was a country road, as much as you can say that about an island road.

And yet called a street, de Groot observed. Like the old Roman roads of England.

And a straight line, too, like those you mentioned, Pendleton said. Only it wasn't a long road, wasn't paved and went nowhere through the spruce trees that I could see. It began at one dead end and ended at another, with a single road from the village meeting it somewhere in between, and maybe a dozen shacks, and not one in sight of the other, along the way. You didn't dare to drive that road because of the dogs sleeping in it, and you didn't like to walk it because of the bullies standing in it, a cigar butt in their mean mouths and their old man's fedora pulled down over their ears. I guess they were supposed to mind the pigs they let loose to forage in the roadside weeds. A haze hung over that street, and I don't believe it was always fog either. More like what you might catch in the Smoky Mountains, which, I assume, is how they came to have that name. But this was more like the smoke of a dump. Or as if peat was burning underneath the leaf cover in the forest. Now, here is the odd piece of information about that street. You could become lost on it even though it went nowhere. Don't ask me how it happened, but it was real easy to turn yourself around so that you faced the wrong way. Which was the beginning of the street, you would ask in your confusion, and which way was the end?

McQuade, who had listened throughout, wondered what this story had to do with anything, much less their present desperate circumstances. Nevertheless, he was interested enough to inquire of de Groot if there were any Smoke Streets where he hailed from; and when he replied, not to his knowledge, McQuade asked him where that was.

I was born in England, de Groot said evasively. Then he corrected himself. Not exactly on the island per se, you understand. But certainly somewhere in the island empire. Then he corrected himself a second time. Actually I wasn't born there either. It was more like Rumania. I may have moved to England as a child. Eventually I made my way to America.

McQuade was unhappy with so contradictory an answer. As he studied de Groot through narrowing eyes, he decided he was the sort to wear a mandarin robe for a dressing gown, along with a mandarin hat; also that in the course of taking a drink, he would instinctively hold his glass up to the light so as to more perfectly examine the transparency and color of the liquor. Just as he was doing now with his whiskey.

Then Fortune was at McQuade's side. You had best rest yourself in preparation for the work ahead, he cautioned. When the time comes for me to acquaint you with the details of my plan, you will learn you play the most important role in the rescue. The freedom of your friend, Sally, depends upon your successful actions. So does the fate of the rest of us. When

Sanderson returns, we will have no time to waste. Every minute will count as much as life itself!

Sanderson had made it safely across the city, only to be halted just short of the embassy gates by a government soldier, a young officer in combat uniform. He said, We are not yet preventing anyone from entering the embassy, our nations are still friendly. As long as yours does not recognize any illegitimate provisional government, we will remain so. How long this will continue depends upon the actions of your government and the course of events in our own unhappy country. The situation, however, could change overnight. Having delivered this statement, he saluted Sanderson and let him pass.

The marine guard at the door knew him by sight and had orders to admit him. It was as though he had been forgiven. He remembered to ask the marine how Mitzi was faring, but instead of answering, the marine made furrows of his forehead and looked away.

The hallways and reception rooms were deserted, and his footsteps echoed across the polished floors. Perhaps the embassy staff was busy behind closed doors, preparing to evacuate, if it came to that. He heard music down the hall. The door to the ambassador's office was ajar; inside, several people were grouped around a phonograph. Sanderson recalled that the ambassador made certain to have his hour of music in the afternoon. Today he had chosen a selection from *Das Rheingold.* A receptionist concentrated on the leitvotivs with her eyes closed. The naval attaché wagged his finger like a metronome before his face. The ambassador pressed his fingertips to his temples as though he had a headache and was smiling bravely with the pain.

Within the dramatic landscapes of the music, black thunderheads were gathering above the hammer Donner swung above his head.

Heda! Heda! Hedo! Donner sang.

Strange coincidence! Out the window, real storm clouds were building up with tremendous speed as they tumbled forward. The room grew dark. The sky became like night. The French horns came in above the swirling strings. Donner's hammer clanged upon the rock. A violent lightning flash and thunderclap. The embassy shook to its foundation. The clouds opened up and the rain poured down. Enough for many days and nights in seconds. A real tropical downpour. Like a hurricane. Or the monsoon. Sanderson had to shut his eyes against the brightness of the flashes, hold his ears to lessen the loudness of the thunder. The rain rolled off the roofs, overflowed the drainpipes, ran like white water in the gutters. Across the countryside, brooks must have swollen, rivers flooded, dams given away, bridges washed out and carried downstream; survivors would be clinging to the rooftops of their floating houses, or rowing in boats down what were once their streets. Sanderson idled on a window seat in the hallway and watched the banana leaves blow about the garden and the surface of the tennis court fill up with puddles.

Then the thunder marched off into the distance,

complaining as it went; the clouds lightened up and separated. The air turned misty; the sun shone through. The banana leaves in the garden were almost hidden by the steam. The birds shook themselves and took to flight. A few raindrops dripped from the eaves.

But did the living earth receive that rain? Sanderson wondered, his forehead pressed against the glass. Or did the storm occur only within the landscapes of some dream?

He found Mitzi in her room. To his surprise, she was no longer bedridden, but sitting up in a chair beside the bed. That was a good sign! And her eyes were open, they were the first thing he noticed. They confronted him when he entered but failed to follow him around the room. Enormous but vacant eyes. Her mouth was set and did not move.

So you have recovered, he said. And sat on the bed beside her, taking her warm but lifeless hand into his own. But what is this, Mitzi? You can sit up all right but you cannot move? And you can see but cannot speak? Nod if this is so.

Her head stayed rigid on her shoulders.

And do you recognize me?

She gave no sign.

We were classmates at school, Mitzi. Both prep school and college. Not so long ago as all that. We went into the mountains once and slept over in a shelter, I can't believe you have forgotten. I may have taken you for a ride in my kayak. It is possible we overturned. I know for a fact I took you canoeing; you were as strong as a man with a paddle. We were often partners in mixed doubles. You were an instinctive player, you knew when to cross over and you volleyed well at the net. Surely some of this must strike a nerve.

She gave him no satisfaction.

Then you leave me no choice but to test you, he said. I must do something that will force you to try and stop me. Perhaps I will go so far as to make you cry out for help.

He went to her dresser and opened the small top drawers with the tiny keys he discovered in a bowl. He put his hands inside the drawers and felt about the underthings. As he did so he faced his own image in the mirror. He popped open a jewelry case and discovered a pair of rings. He held them up to the light and saw himself reduced and fractured in the tiny stones. As though he were trapped inside that sparkle. He wondered if Mitzi had watched him in the mirror. He turned and displayed the rings, one between the thumb and index finger of either hand. Was he mistaken, or had her eyes moved ever so slightly while his back was turned? Prepare yourself, this is a test, he said. Watch me closely. And he put the rings in his pocket.

Then he remembered the ring that she was wearing. Again he took her hand affectionately, then separated her ring finger from the others and wiggled the band free, working it up and down against the flesh until it slipped along the bone. He paused. This is how criminals behave, he told himself. Or worse than criminals. Nevertheless, his behavior fascinated him and made him tremble.

Impulsively he set his mouth around her finger; how warm it was. He gripped the ring between his teeth, keeping his lips flush against her flesh. He felt her nail flick against his palate. Gently he tugged the metal band over the joint and wrinkles. He had the uncanny sense that she was gazing down on him as he worked, her eyes moving as eerily and unnaturally as a statue's eyes. Frightened, he paused momentarily in his effort, his head buried in her hand. Then he had the ring off the nail and free in his mouth, where it rested on his tongue before he let it fall into his hand.

His job done, he stood up and kissed her once while gazing openly into her eyes, which were as astonished as his own.

Now you know who I am, he said.

McQuade wondered what was taking Sanderson so long. It was nerve-racking, sitting helplessly in the Seafarers and waiting for his return. Unnoticed by the others, he wandered out into the streets. He imagined their consternation and was amused. McQuade has disappeared! they would shout. All is lost! Well, what did they know? He could look after himself; he knew what he was about. Not a light was showing from the streetlights and buildings. So true a blackout that he thought the electricity had been lost. He did not encounter lights until he stumbled upon the small alley lined with noisy night spots. He descended into a cabaret below the level of the street.

The little club was packed with revelers celebrating frantically as though emigration or death awaited them tomorrow. Their abandon reminded him of Mardi Gras or New Year's Eve. Some wore evening dress along with eye masks and party hats. There were even a few harlequins and Punchinellos. A man in black tie and tails was busy pulling down the streamers that were draped around the room. The city is surrounded! he shouted. There is no escape! He had a waxed mustache and his hair was parted in the middle of his head.

Above the crush of frantic dancers, a jazz band of old musicians in white tuxedos was playing on a small stage. A black piano player, but a saxophone player who resembled McQuade's father in the way he combed his hair. One of the party at McQuade's table said the band had just returned from a successful tour of the Yucatán, and that the singer was La Flamme, an American girl, fresh from the States. Her voice sounded familiar to McQuade. She picked him out of the crowd and kept her eyes on him as she sang:

Love, your melody is in the air
Yet I call you and you are not there
Come, here is my heart, my soul to mate
Make me forget the voice that whispers, Wait!

When the song was finished, she came down from the stage and forced her way to McQuade's table. You are McQuade, she said. You have been here before.

McQuade said, Déjà vu!

I know a joke, the singer said. On a napkin she

wrote out, Isle of View. Now read it back to me, she said.

I love you, said McQuade.

Poor boy, the singer said, and I love you, too! She squeezed his cheeks between her hands and kissed him so hard his lips were forced back to fill the spaces between his teeth. Laughing, she ran through the portiere of beads that led backstage.

By the time McQuade found his way back to the Seafarers, Sanderson had arrived before him. He had already delivered Mitzi's three rings to Fortune, who had examined them and slapped their bearer on the back, declaring them to be the most satisfactory rings he had ever seen.

As soon as McQuade took his place beside the others around the table, in the center of which stood the bottle of whiskey and the lighted candle, Fortune said, Here is our plan. He drew with a pencil on the map that was unfolded in their midst. Gabriella will return to the apartment where I found her, which is here, on the edge of Smoke Street. I will take the rings and go to the central army barracks. When I have secured the release of Sally, I will take her to Gabriella's place, which is only a few blocks in this direction. In the meantime, McQuade and Sanderson will return to the embassy. There you will arrange to do two things. You will have a car sent from the embassy to Gabriella's, where it will pick up Gabriella, myself and Sally. Secondly—and this is most important—

you must arrange to have a motorboat waiting at the docks to take us all out to your ship anchored in the harbor, aboard which we will make good our escape. The embassy car will drive us to the motorboat, where you two will, of course, be awaiting our arrival. On the docks you will be reunited with your sweetheart, think on that, McQuade!

Fortune would be the first to leave. Followed by Gabriella. Not long afterward, Sanderson and McQuade were to head for the embassy, one at a time.

Before Fortune left, Sanderson took him aside. I should go with you, he said.

In so dangerous an enterprise, Fortune said, one head is safer than two.

Then let me go with Gabriella, he said. She should not have to walk the streets alone. I can wait with her at her apartment.

Why do you make such offers? Fortune wondered. Are you afraid that, once we are out of your sight, we will run off with the rings and renege on our promise to rescue McQuade's girl friend?

Sanderson had never entertained these suspicions. However, he said nothing in his own defense.

Even if your suspicions were justified, Fortune said, you would still have to accompany McQuade. He can't be trusted to carry out your part of the plan alone. He puts up a brave front, but the man is either injured or ill. Haven't you noticed how his eyes roll back inside his head? His behavior is unpredictable, he acts impulsively. He doesn't consider the consequences. You heard how he snuck out to a cabaret just now and lost all track of time. I ask you, is that any way for the man to behave? We can't put our lives in the hands of such a man. Nor can we leave him to blunder about on his own.

Sanderson acknowledged the truth of these remarks. He had himself reached the same conclusion about McQuade.

Before Fortune slipped out the back way, Sanderson observed him approach McQuade and say, Forget your pains! Stay awake! We depend on you!

When it was the turn of Gabriella to leave, she maneuvered Sanderson into a corner. Why return to the embassy with McQuade? she whispered. Why not come with me instead? And she placed her hands upon his chest.

It was what Sanderson had wanted most to happen. He would go with her in a minute if it were not for the unpredictability of McQuade! I will be in the car that comes for you from the embassy, he said. In gratitude, he seized her hands and brought them to his lips.

But you don't dare return to the embassy, she said. Or have you forgotten about the rings?

Of course, the rings! He had forgotten about those rings. And so, apparently, had Fortune. He was certain he had told Fortune he had as good as stolen them, and yet here was Fortune, returning him to the scene of the crime. If the burglary were discovered and the blame laid to Sanderson, the ambassador would hardly agree to put an embassy car at the disposal of the suspected thief, or help in his arrangements to escape aboard a ship. Nor, by showing up in the company of McQuade, did Sanderson want to risk implicating his friend in the theft. And Fortune had worried about trusting the judgment of McQuade! Sanderson wondered if he should have trusted Fortune.

I will come with you, Sanderson said.

Keep me a block ahead of you at all times, she said. Never lose sight of me.

You there, McQuade, Sanderson said, turning to his friend. Can you carry on alone?

I feel like I can do anything, McQuade answered.

You can't afford to make a mistake, Sanderson cautioned.

I made it to the embassy before without your help, and, count on it, I will make it there again, McQuade said.

But McQuade decided not to go immediately to the embassy. He sat down to save his strength and rest up for the next stage of the adventure. Thank goodness, he had Sanderson and Fortune helping him out. Taking his place, as it were. Extensions of himself, you might say.

While Pendleton and de Groot were busy packing notebooks, sorting through correspondence and burning files, McQuade shut his eyes and saw himself in the Dakotas, tramping the road beneath the orange sky. The same dirt road winding through the darkness as before, dusty underfoot. He hadn't seen a car since setting out; hadn't passed a lighted house for miles. When he identified the farmhouse by its single blunted light that bespoke the kitchen, he broke into a run. Inside, he would find his hiding place. He tore open the screen door and ran up the narrow stairs into the breathless attic where he picked his way among the old mannequins and stacks of *National Geographics*. Orange light filtered through the one small dusty window. The heat was like a kiln.

Downstairs, the screen door banged. Followed by footsteps walking through the rooms. Now someone was playing the piano in the parlor. "Sweet Lorraine" at first. Followed by the famous "Palm Room Serenade," the theme song of his father when he played the supper hour at the downtown Milwaukee hotel. Father, he said. The piano ceased. Footsteps came up the stairs, cautiously, and stopped before the attic door. The knob was tried without success.

McQuade found an old C-melody saxophone, which he hung around his neck. Then he located an old cane and hobbled on it to the door, surprised at how lame he had become. When he threw open the door, the cane was poised to strike above his head.

His father confronted him in the darkened doorway. Again the white dinner jacket and black tie, the shiny stripes down the sides of his trousers; his hair was slicked back over his head. So once again you return to the beginning, he said. Hiding on the farm won't keep you from being caught, when will you learn? You should be glad I found you first. Before the "other side." And he winked as though McQuade understood the significance of this remark. How many times must you be told you can't return to your own beginning, he said, never mind a beginning as remote as mine. For example, that saxophone around your neck was not yours but mine. And that was your grandfather's cane. If you carried this going backward far enough, you would find yourself reversed into an amoeba. You might be reduced to the essential elements themselves. Or return to light, which, as the good book says, was first of all. Why not abandon these delaying tactics and give up the ghost?

His father had made one point, anyway; McQuade could concede that much. It could be as dangerous to go too far ahead in your trip toward the end as it was to stay behind in the beginning. One had to know exactly how far to remove oneself, for safety's sake.

Whenever you are ready, his father said, I will take you home.

But McQuade, leaning on the cane, tried to push past him, the saxophone swinging against his chest. His father tried to stop him. He placed himself in his path. He said, I told you I won't let you start fresh again. I mean to do everything in my power to make you take up where you left off instead.

In reply, McQuade gave him a little shove. His father returned the shove, and then some.

McQuade thought, He doesn't know how to comfort me. He can't bring himself at this late hour to apologize. He doesn't know how to be my friend. Even so, he said, Father, I am sorry for my part in this affair. Give me your hand.

Come now, none of that, his father said. No need to discuss it further, it is time to go.

But instead of letting himself be led off, McQuade brandished the cane and backed his father down the stairs. Then McQuade decided, why not, he would chase him through the rooms, one by one. Both of them were wild and shouting. Finally they had it out in the yard beside the broken windmill, two silhouettes circling and threatening each other against the backdrop of that orange sky.

His father removed his dinner jacket, rolled up his sleeves and struck a boxing pose. He said, A son always rebels against his father. If you were to live a bit longer, you might discover that the old man wasn't such a dimwit after all.

McQuade poked him in the chest with the tip of the cane. Then he raised it as though to strike a blow. I'm going to give you such a licking, you naughty man, he said.

Hold on, his father said. Answer me, who is the father here and who is the son?

McQuade struggled with the cane; his arm was shaking. It was as though the stick were alive with a powerful will of its own. Defeated, McQuade lowered the cane. I am sorry, Father, he said for the second time. Give me your hand.

His father took it this time. We have both lost our youth, he said. You in your way, and I in mine. Some might say we are nearly equals now.

McQuade pulled his father to himself as he might a smaller, slighter boy. It was as if he had overtaken his father, had made the old man eat his dust.

Together they went into the fields, his father indicating the horizon of orange above the black as though to tell him that was where he rightfully belonged and where they would join forces on the day that the father became the equal of the son.

I saw my father just now, McQuade said to de Groot, who was stuffing papers and money into an open satchel. This makes the second time, for I saw him earlier.

A man thinks of his family at such an hour, de Groot said. Pendleton, for example.

Across the room Pendleton was methodically using a ruler to tear up the contents of several files.

He is a widower, de Groot said, lowering his voice. And a father who has outlived his children. He had five of them once, but they are gone now, all his little boys and girls. When they died, his wife died, too. She killed them. This took place in winter in a graveyard down the road from where they lived. She made them lie down in the snow, and then she shot them, one by one. When she was finished with them, she turned the rifle on herself. She was mentally ill, of course. She heard an irrepressible voice that urged her to destroy herself and all her children. The doctors had released her from the state hospital on the condition that she continue to take a medication that would prevent her from yielding to such a voice. This drug worked so well that she pronounced herself cured. And if she was cured—or so her reasoning went—why should she continue the medication? Pendleton was far from home at the time of the tragedy, and in no position to know what she was doing.

As if Pendleton had been listening to this account, he now sat idle with his elbows on the desk, a look of suffering and nostalgia on his face. As though in his thoughts he had returned to that earlier and more familiar time of his small island off the coast of Maine with its whitewashed lighthouse, stacks of weathered lobster traps before the fishing shacks and a white-steepled church where, after singing the old-fashioned hymns, the congregation would exit into the foggy road.

De Groot had himself grown contemplative. Perhaps he saw himself boarding the small Orient-Pacific liner on which he had booked passage to some lonely outpost in the China Sea where he would again change names and nationality; or as he scurried in the rain along some gas-lit Amsterdam canal while the women in the windows above the diamond shops observed his progress in their mirrors; or as he crossed a crowded bazaar, his broad panama afloat among a sea of fezes. Eventually he started out of this dream state and, surprised to find McQuade still in their company, urged him to hurry; already he was late; he had to go.

The large straw hat that had disguised McQuade so well on his previous walk to the embassy was again on his head as he set out on his new journey across the city. One did not abandon a good thing. This time he encountered broken glass and spent cartridges in the streets along with heaps of burning refuse and a few burned-out cars and buses. Fortunately, the shooting had become sporadic and was occurring in some other quarter of the city. He had gone only a few blocks when he became uncertain of the way. The streets looked so different now that the shops were boarded up. Why hadn't he brought along de Groot's map that had guided him so faithfully before? Which way was he to go? Across the street, a group of soldiers was observing his indecision. They rested their rifle butts on the pavement while their hands gripped the barrels. In the same instant that McQuade started toward them with the intention of asking directions, they waved him over to their checkpoint. Before he could open his mouth, one of the soldiers lifted the sombrero from his head, while the others looked him over front and back. He did not look like themselves, one said. He was not one of them, said another. Why then was he trying to look like them when, clearly, he was something else? They examined the straw hat. Was he a spy? wondered a third. The soldier appeared to be their leader. He had thick lips and wide front teeth which the hairs of his mustache almost covered. He informed the others that the appearance of McQuade was suspicious and unsatisfactory. You will come with us, he ordered.

McQuade protested. It's important that I reach the American Embassy, he said.

Get going, a soldier said.

You have no right, I am an American citizen, lives are at stake, insisted McQuade.

Move it, the soldier said.

McQuade was marched off to the infamous central police headquarters and made to sit on a hard bench. The plaster wall behind him was full of bullet holes. His interrogation was conducted by a curious army colonel, who happened to be in the building, and no less than the district police chief himself. The chief wore a double-breasted suit with wide lapels and high-heeled cowboy boots. The colonel's tunic was unbuttoned, revealing his bare chest; his pants were dusty, but McQuade could see reflections in his boots. Both men had curly black hair and pencil stripes for mustaches. McQuade tried to explain how he had to reach the American Embassy, it was a matter of life and death. He showed them his papers, fumbling with them as he unfolded them and set them out upon the desk.

The colonel, enjoying his cigarette, scoffed at this display. He was perched on the corner of the police chief's desk. You could be a Canadian, pretending to be an American, he said, his head thrown back, blowing the smoke straight up as though from a chimney. How would we know?

Tell us the name of the American baseball team with the most Latin-American ballplayers on its roster, asked the chief of police.

San Diego? McQuade guessed. San Francisco?

Ha! You are an American and you don't know that, and you expect us to believe you?

Är ni Svensk? asked the colonel.

What is the capital of Savannah? said the chief of police.

Are you CIA or FBI? demanded the colonel.

Such a barrage of questions only served to rattle McQuade until he became too tongue-tied and frightened to answer. Am I on trial? he complained.

What gives you that idea? the police chief said. It would be presumptuous to judge you, we have no such power. Execute you, however, that is a different matter.

We are getting nowhere, the colonel said. Suppose you simply tell us in your own words what you have been doing since your arrival in our country. Exactly as it happened. Leave out nothing. Begin at the beginning.

Men have a way of beginning, the police chief said. And, oddly enough, of ending. He was much amused by his own remark.

McQuade was too confused to lie. Besides, he saw no reason not to tell the truth. That is, up until the moment he and his friends had made their plans to rescue Sally; he would say nothing of that. He would insist he was making his way to the embassy so as to save himself from all this anarchy and insurrection. Other than that, he would give them so much truth that it could not help but confuse them. He began with his first day ashore.

During his recounting of these events, he became aware that the station was filling up with street urchins. Many were barefoot; some had lottery tickets pinned to their shirtfronts; others carried shoeshine kits. McQuade wondered if those boys who came and went in a steady stream ran messages for the police or were informers. And if those who sat around loitering had themselves been captured concealing ammunition or running guns.

One moment, the police chief said, interrupting McQuade when he was far along in his story. We have let too much of your fairy tale go unchallenged in the mistaken hope that you would soon clarify your many cloudy points and particulars. The time has come to ask unpleasant questions.

The time has come to pin you down, the colonel said. You see, I am confused. You were in our city where you were waylaid and robbed and probably beaten, and then you were at the farmhouse in the Dakotas or somewhere with your dear father and mother—how nice—and then you were back in our country at this place you refuse to name but which I think must be called "Seafarers"—as if we haven't heard of it before. I do not understand this, not a word of it, not at all.

An exasperated police chief said, And then and then and then. But then when? What time is then? Is it a time before or after the given incident you recollected earlier? Did the time when you were in your embassy take place before or after the time at the farmhouse, never mind the delightful if melancholic interlude in the mountain village where you lost your horses. You see what I am driving at? This "and then" element presupposes, doesn't it, the presence of a clock moving forward as we know it. Tick-tock. And how odd that at the same time you move forward you have this frozen scene of the orange sky and black earth, a crazy business. Let me explain this from the listener's point of view. It is as if you are imposing a film on a still photograph, or is it vice versa? And making us watch them superimposed, the one moving on, incoherently, to be sure, and the other standing still. For example, when exactly did this happen with your family on the farm?

It happened, as I said, at night, McQuade replied.

Nothing more definite than the darkness? You wouldn't go so far as to say February? You couldn't bring yourself to identify a particular year of our Lord?

The colonel slid off the desk and stood with one booted foot on a chair. We won't accuse you of lying, but you must admit, my friend, he said, blowing smoke, that the world in your story works differently from the real world of the here and now, of we three men meeting at this hour in this room. You manipulate times and places—not to mention people—as it suits your secret purpose. You refuse to allow the clock to be that immutable, irrefutable and, yes, comfortable vehicle that backs up your testimony from one happening to the next, from place to place, from beginning to end. Ah, he was pleased with the way that he was putting it. The smoking cigarette wagged up and down in his mouth as he delivered his phrases.

The police chief took a slightly different tack. How can we believe your story if you are unwilling, or unable, to distinguish the true from the false within its framework, he posed; what actually happened and what was only imagined to have happened; what you have experienced and what exists only in your mind; what is real and what is fantasy? If you cannot make such distinctions, what hope is there for your listeners?

You must think you can live your life in some magic time machine, the colonel said. You step inside, and right away you pull all the levers. You not only voyage through space, like your average airplane, but you take a trip through time as well.

But McQuade thought, Life isn't my testimony. It isn't a story. It isn't being told by anyone. It is actually happening before our astonished eyes. Whereas what I am telling them has already happened, and because they didn't witness those occurrences, they can only learn about them from another party. A witness. A storyteller. Myself. Naturally I am bound to have some faults and failings, who hasn't? And to take some liberties and license, what do they expect? I can't remember everything. Sometimes, during the blank spots, I have to fill in and flesh out. I probably interpret almost as much as I report. It's all colored by my character. I mean, they have to reckon with the likes of me. But he spoke none of these thoughts in his own defense.

The colonel had run out of patience. Try again, he ordered. And this time keep your time frame ordered and explicit, we insist. And hurry up about it, too. Pretend that all this time you talk about is in your hands and burning like a bonfire. You are of two minds about this fire. You want to cup it and protect it from being blown out by any passing wind, for you have no desire to go in darkness, but on the other hand, the fire burns into your flesh—it hurts like hell!

Frightened, McQuade talked as fast as he could.

But again he must have made no sense to his interrogators, for they ordered him to remain silent while they took counsel within his hearing in a corner across the room.

With this fellow, it is all nightmares and nonsense, the colonel said. Or do you think he could be faking?

I think he is loco, answered the chief of police. He tells the truth, all right, when he says he was hit on the head. As far as I am concerned, he belongs to your department. Deal with him as you like.

Just then McQuade remembered Sanderson, Gabriella and Fortune, and the part of the plan he was to perform in the rescue of Sally and, immediately afterwards, in their escape aboard his ship. It was all he could do not to tear his hair and throw himself against the walls. I demand to see a representative of my government! he said.

Instead of agreeing to this request, the colonel had him put in a cell, where he continued to shout that they should bring him a representative from his own country. The guards said they had had just about enough of all this shouting. They forced McQuade into the farthest corner of his cell by prodding him with their rifle butts, which they inserted between the bars.

But this did not stop McQuade from shouting.

* * *

Sanderson had followed Gabriella into Smoke Street. Or so he surmised. Or if not yet Smoke Street, certainly the outskirts of that district. Narrow streets of tenements with grillwork balconies that almost touched overhead, with cement-colored facades pock-marked with the many hits from shells and bullets, unrepaired over a half-century of revolutions. Almost no one was on the streets. A stout woman shuffled at a dogtrot down the sidewalk, hauling water in a terra-cotta jug. A block ahead, a young girl could be seen running, carrying a loaf of bread. Sanderson caught sight of faces in some of the upper-story windows of the buildings; they were like the faces of dead men propped up against the glass. A few soldiers were posted as lookouts on the rooftops, where they resembled gargoyles, squatting on the eaves. Ahead, Gabriella passed through a gateway into a park. Sanderson quickened his pace and followed.

Such a strange park, like nothing Sanderson had ever seen. A square of dusty greenery enclosed on all sides by blocks of tenements, and in its center, a tremendous outcrop of rock several stories high and overgrown with jungle vines and foliage. A natural formation, Sanderson wondered, or the ruins of an ancient temple? The crumbling, sand-colored rock, where it was exposed, was a honeycomb of tunnels, while the vegetation exploded with the sudden movements of screaming birds and monkeys. A large excavation site, many feet deep, was roped off at the base of the rock.

As soon as Sanderson had caught up to Gabriella, he pulled her close to him. In response, she put her face against his chest, her ear pressed against the panic of his heart.

I no longer love him, she said.

I knew that intuitively, he answered. The first time you looked at me, you showed me that.

What you have lost you must leave, she said.

How fortunate she made him feel! She was in his arms; he had known it would come to that. At the same time, he felt weighted by the inevitability and somberness of tragedy, as though she had committed him to some dreadful enterprise whose outcome he could not escape. You make me believe we can be safe in such a place, he lied, whispering.

To live without love is to cheat, she said, following her own thoughts.

Listen to my heart beat, he replied.

Is that love? she wondered.

Fear and love, he confessed. And it is torture, all in one.

Already you love me? she asked.

He nodded.

Tell me about your love, she said. Is it the kind that eats you inside out?

It must be that, he answered.

Is it like crawling on your hands and knees, she said, and groping for me—or for someone like me—in the dark? Do you know what I mean?

Sanderson shook his head.

What is the best thing you do? she asked.

Sanderson was at a loss. Is it making love? he stammered.

No, feeling love, she corrected. And what is the best thing you have done?

He thought about this, but nothing came easily to his mind. It seems I have yet to do it, he answered.

Do it soon!

Yes, you are right, of course, he answered, and rested his head on her shoulder. How tired he was; he was becoming as feeble as McQuade. What had happened to his willpower? Where was his self-control? She must love me, he said to himself. And the love is worth as much as my life. It is worth more, even.

She said, When Fortune sent his messages from the countryside, I sent his messengers away. This made him believe that I had disappeared. He put his life in danger when he came in search of me. That must not happen again.

The truth will break his heart when he learns it, Sanderson said to himself.

This time he must not go in search of me, she said. And if he does go, he must not find me. But even if he finds me, he will not recognize me, I will have changed so much—I will look like someone he never knew! She kissed Sanderson. But when he attempted to return the kiss, she offered him her cheek. You must take care of yourself, she said. From this moment on, you are on your own.

Sanderson was incredulous. Have I come with you only to be left alone? he asked.

I must leave before he returns, she said. You must

be on hand to tell him the truth. And do not let him follow me, no matter what else he does.

I have an idea, Sanderson said. It is a good idea. We will go together. Let him receive the news from others.

And what will become of your friends? she said. She pointed out the windows of her rooms in the gray building across the street and handed him the key. You know as well as I do, she said, you must stay there and help them when they come.

He was overwhelmed by a sense of unhappiness and goodness at work within him, both at once. I can't stand this, he said. I have this premonition you will be alive long after I am dead.

In response, she drew away from him.

The way you look at me, he said. It tells me I am doomed. You must tell me that I will survive this—you must encourage me!

We will meet again, she said.

Do you promise? He was afraid to ask her where and when.

I promise.

Swear it then!

On my grave, she said.

If I die in this business, he warned, I will come back for you.

To haunt me? she said.

To fetch you! he countered. If I can't live without you, don't expect me to die without you. I will find you no matter where you are. Even if your trail leads to places like Haiti and the Congo, I will follow. Don't expect the sight of me to be pleasant. I will probably be a corpse, or ghost. I will be passionate, however!

Do it then! she said.

And she ran away from him across the park and vanished in the streets.

In the police headquarters the army colonel accompanied by several soldiers came for McQuade and released him from his cell. If you have prayers to offer, say them now, McQuade said to himself.

You wanted to see your countrymen, the colonel said; well, some of your countrymen have come to see you.

Americans? McQuade asked eagerly.

Your countrymen! the colonel repeated.

The soldiers snickered.

They're not prisoners themselves? McQuade asked, suspiciously.

I assure you, no one restrains them.

This time the soldiers burst out laughing. One went so far as to slap his knee.

And from the embassy?

You bet they are from the embassy, the colonel said. And they bring a message to you from home.

Home! McQuade thought. It meant baseball and firecrackers and lilies of the valley and cheeseburgers and a can of Simonize and a girl friend posing for a snapshot on the fender of a secondhand car.

With the colonel in the lead, McQuade was escorted down a corridor that gradually descended and intersected other corridors, with small electric lights burning every thirty yards or so along the route. McQuade thought they must be entering some command headquarters or dungeon underground. Finally they emerged into a honeycomb of chambers where there was dirt and dampness and a horrible stench. It was as though the place had been mined out of a graveyard and the surrounding putrefaction was seeping through the walls. He was led into a cell where a pair of skeletons in moldy uniforms was seated on wooden chairs. They appeared to have been shot where they sat, for they were tied to the chair backs with loops of rotten rope that, even now, kept them fixed to their seats. This is the cruelest joke, McQuade said to himself.

After a while the colonel said, Well, now, what do you say to your countrymen's offer?

Offer? McQuade said, terrified. What offer?

Aren't they making you an offer?

If they are, McQuade answered, I haven't heard it.

The colonel lit a cigarette. He held it so that the balls of his four fingers and his thumb touched it at once. In other words, you refuse to talk to them, he said. You can hear me very well, but you can't hear them. He had taken his pistol out of his holster and was walking about with it loosely in his hand.

Just then a senior officer passed by the cell, sorting through a handful of papers as he walked. He was in stocking feet, and his suspenders could be seen beneath his unbuttoned tunic. He was scratching his stomach.

Pardon me, your excellency, the colonel said. Our young American friend is proving obstinate. He refuses to speak with his countrymen. He goes so far as to deny they are even speaking to him. As you know, I am unable to speak or understand so difficult a tongue. He pointed to the corpses and their hideous grins.

The senior officer removed his sunglasses and peered first at the colonel and then at McQuade. You want me to interpret?

If you would, your excellency.

You think I can understand them then?

The colonel laughed. If you will, he said.

The senior officer continued to shuffle through his papers, pausing every now and then to skim a page as he stood before the pair of skeletons seated in the chairs. After a while, he said, I see. That is how it is, is it? Good. I understand. He repeated, I understand. He turned to the colonel. They say it is not necessary that he accompany them to their embassy. They are willing to permit him to remain with us in our pleasant little country after all. It is their opinion that no matter where he is, he is still within their jurisdiction, protected by their laws. It is a technical point, difficult to understand. But for them it is all that matters. By the way, they do not understand why, as their countryman, he does not look more like themselves.

Some countryman, the colonel said. Perhaps he should be made to look more like his own kind.

The senior officer, still engrossed in his papers, started to walk away. As an afterthought, he said, For Americans, they were unusually eloquent.

There, the colonel said to McQuade, your countrymen have made you a reasonable offer. Please have the courtesy and good sense to accept it. Stay here with them or depart in their company, it makes no difference to them, and is all the same to you.

When they had tired of their fun, they led McQuade back to his cell.

Gabriella's small apartment was like a suite of rooms in an abandoned hotel. The high ceilings had come down in places, the plaster walls were cracked and tiles had lifted from the floor. Like a place of assignation, or a way station in some journey of escape across the city, that was what Sanderson thought of the place. What if you died in such a setting? he said to himself. And he threw himself facedown on the unmade bed.

Luckily he did not have to wait long before Fortune was at the door. Victory, he said, and put his finger to his lips. He had not come alone. But instead of Sally, he had brought, inexplicably, a small government soldier in uniform who was in such a weakened condition that he had to be helped into the apartment and onto the bed. As soon as this was accomplished, Fortune registered the presence of the man who had greeted him. Sanderson! he said. Why didn't you accompany McQuade?

Sanderson could not meet his gaze.

Never mind, Fortune said, placing his hands on Sanderson's shoulders, I understand. You changed the plan because you thought it was your duty to protect Gabriella. Unfortunately, you have endangered her life with your gallantry. You have endangered all our lives. Why would you entrust our lives to a man like McQuade?

Before Sanderson could reply, Fortune, looking alarmed, hurried into the adjoining parlor. And where is Gabriella? he demanded, confronting the empty rooms.

Sanderson, who had dreaded such a moment, could not bring himself to speak the truth. You were gone too long, he said. She feared for the worst. You were trapped in some building she said. Or maybe you were arrested. She claimed she could intuit these things. The first time I turned my back, she gave me the slip.

For a moment Fortune seemed to lose his nerve. Sanderson was certain he had read the words, Done for! on his lips.

When Fortune had composed himself, he said, The streets have never been so dangerous. Where do I look for her first?

Alarmed, Sanderson said, You were to wait here until she returned. She made me promise that I would keep you with me.

She went in search of me, Fortune answered, and

you expect me not to do the same for her? He spoke contemptuously.

Sanderson did not know how to answer this.

Before Fortune left, he went to the bed and addressed the little soldier. We are here, he whispered. Halfway home. He unbuttoned the soldier's tunic, and a woman's blouse was revealed beneath. He removed the helmet, and a mass of blond hair was released. He parted the hair with his hands, and, to the astonishment of Sanderson, the face of a young woman was revealed. Sally! True to his word, Fortune had rescued her!

She is in surprisingly good condition, Fortune pronounced. She has a strong heart and a brave spirit. Isn't that so, Sally? But in an aside to Sanderson, he whispered, How much she has been through, and yet how wonderful she looks. McQuade is luckier than he deserves, or knows.

But Sanderson was not listening. He was at the window where he was aware, for the first time, of that eerie sound sent up like smoke or heat shimmers from the sunbaked city. Such a secret sound, bespeaking ritual and mystery. It perplexed and stunned him until he felt as slow and ponderous as when he saw himself floundering in his attempt to flee the source of danger in a dream. A distant murmuring. A chanting. Dronelike. Dirgelike. As though he heard surf from a long way off. Or the wingbeats of blackbirds swarming in their dusky clouds within the leafless trees. It might have passed for the roar of a football crowd in some stadium outside the city. Except that he could detect fear in those voices. Also, agony. And lamentation. It was the outcry of multitudes heard only as a whisper. It chilled Sanderson's soul. What is that? he asked Fortune who, himself shaken by the sound, had joined him at the window.

The sound of the siege, Fortune answered. The cries of the killers and of those they are about to kill. In that moment, the one is as terrified as the other. His hand pointed out the bell tower of a Spanish-style mission surrounded by a grove of palms. It comes from there, he said. The rebels have begun the assault of Smoke Street and are advancing in our direction. The troops of the notorious General Faustino are spearheading the attack. They have lived so long in the mountains, they are barely human. They will take a terrible vengeance in this district where so many of their comrades have suffered horribly. The government soldiers are as nervous as monkeys; I wouldn't count on them to stand and fight. If they hear so much as a rumor of a breakthrough, they will throw down their arms and run for their lives. You may witness their retreat yourself. God help the civilians left behind at such an hour!

What is the best escape route? Sanderson asked, alarmed.

If the worst happens, Fortune said, and McQuade does not return in time to take you out, make use of this. And he handed him a small vial, corked at the top. Here is your best way out.

Sanderson studied the object in his palm, his hand trembling. How has it come to this? he asked himself. Nothing in his past had prepared him for so alien an undertaking. Surely that which was happening was never intended to be a portion of his life. It was as though he had been maneuvered into taking the place of another. Fortune, perhaps. Or, more likely, McQuade. As though from now on he counted for nothing and was the stand-in for McQuade. And to the brink of death, apparently. This is the only way? he asked.

No, but it is the best way, Fortune answered. You don't want to hear about the other ways. The vial contains the deadliest of poisons, but you guessed that much. It has no antidote. The Indians of the rain forests extract it from the roots of a plant that grows only in their region. They use it in their sacrifices and ceremonies. Even the smallest drop is quick-acting and proves fatal, so make certain to give Sally a dose before you take your own. You need only to raise her head and pour the drops into her mouth. They say your lips go numb as soon as the poison touches them. You are paralyzed before you can feel the pain.

Fortune made a final examination of Sally. Asleep already, he said. She looks a picture. Let her rest until it is time to go.

On the stairs he said, If McQuade comes, tell him to wait for me and Gabriella as long as he thinks it is safe. But just in case you are left in the lurch and think you still have an opportunity to escape, I have this to give you.

What is it this time, Sanderson thought, dismally, a penknife to open my veins?

Instead, Fortune produced two of Mitzi's rings. Sanderson recognized them immediately. It only cost me one to ransom her, Fortune said. These two I kept back. Take one for yourself, you may need it to bribe a soldier.

With the ring in his pocket, Sanderson felt only a little bit less hopeless. He thought, Now, at least, I may have an alternative to administering the poison.

With Fortune gone, Sanderson turned his attention to Sally. Again her hair had become twisted in front of her face. He brushed it aside and barely recognized the face he saw as that of the same Sally he had seen in the mountain village. He was appalled by her pallor. What did Fortune mean, claiming she looked a picture? She had suffered terribly; you could read little else upon her face. Surely she was ill or injured. What else explained her fever, her erratic breathing? Minutes appeared to pass before he could detect any movement of her lungs. He felt for her pulse but was afraid he heard only the rush of his own frightened heart. He said to himself, You had best come quick, McQuade.

McQuade found soldiers in the streets around the embassy, piling sandbags along the curbs. Tanks patrolled the area and had their cannon trained in opposite directions, so that it was unclear whether they were positioned to defend the embassy or assault it. When McQuade showed the ticket of safe passage given him by the chief of police who had detained him, the soldiers let him through their cordon, and the marine guards let him through the gate. It was then that he made himself believe he had been delayed for so long a time in the prison that his friends, weary of waiting for him, had made their way to the embassy on their own. Think of it, Sally and Sanderson just inside these doors, ready to greet him. Fortune and Gabriella, also.

Instead, he was confronted by the ambassador and naval attaché, who had received word of his coming. Before he could do more than shake their hands, the naval attaché said, What has your friend done with the rings?

Immediately McQuade felt like a small child caught unexpectedly in a lie. He had completely forgotten that Sanderson, when he had been here earlier, had stolen those rings! And so had Fortune forgotten, apparently. None of them had foreseen that the burglary would be discovered this soon, or that Sanderson would be suspected.

A nice job Sanderson has pulled off, the naval attaché said, pacing the floor. Nothing but a second-story man, a common burglar.

Well, I should say a kind of Raffles, the ambassador suggested. You know, coming from the best family and level of society that he does. And then using his secure position here as a houseguest to case the place.

You can never forgive such an abuse of hospitality, the attaché said. We count at least three rings missing.

He must have had his reasons for taking them, the ambassador said. And, who knows, perhaps he has already put them to good use. You see, I continue, despite so much evidence to the contrary, to have faith in my fellowman. Nevertheless, these rings do not belong to Sanderson, and he must be made to return them. Mitzi should not have to suffer this new loss in her life. Especially now, when she was showing every sign of recovering from the effects of her earlier disappointment. I should like you to persuade your friend to return the rings; there is no good denying you know he has them.

McQuade thought fast. He was aware that he must soon ask the ambassador for a favor, two favors, really. You have asked the right man, he said. I will do what I can.

No questions asked upon their receipt, the ambassador added. Or beforehand, for that matter.

Agreed, McQuade said.

It's a good thing you didn't try to defend your friend, the naval attaché said, a bit smugly. The marine guard at the gate saw him sneak in and out of the building. We knew the rings were in the room before he entered and were missing after he left, with no one else entering in the interim. What you would call an open-and-shut case.

At this point McQuade thought it best to explain that the rings were needed to ransom Sally Sunstrum, his own friend, and an American like themselves; also to acquaint them with the plight of his four friends waiting in the apartment across the city to be rescued by a car dispatched from the embassy under the direction of McQuade.

But the ambassador put up his hand before he could get out so much as a word. No questions asked, he said, remember our agreement? I said it, and I mean to keep my word.

And with that, he left the room.

Mitzi will want to see you, I am sure, the naval attaché said. Maybe she will listen to your story.

He escorted McQuade upstairs to the doors of Mitzi's bedroom, where he had been before, and left him there. Mitzi lay in her nightgown atop the satin bedspread; her eyes were closed. How beautiful and coiffured she looked, as though she had just been visited in secret by her hairdresser and cosmetician. And how cool and aloof besides, so that a man caressing her might well imagine he was fondling porcelain. Now was his chance, McQuade told himself. Instead of rousing her, he responded to an old urge and lay down beside her on the bed. The mattress yielded beneath his weight, and the bedclothes shifted. How soft it was. He couldn't say why he did it, except that he was tired, the bed was inviting, the space was there, and he didn't think she would catch him at it if he lay quite still and only used the bed for a little while. He shut his eyes. Such a weariness and weakness he was feeling.

When he was next aware of his surroundings, Mitzi was awake beside him. She had turned on her side and was reclining with her head resting on her elbow so that she could study him. The neckline of her gown was loosened by such a pose, revealing the upper portions of her breasts with the one resting on the other. She held up her ring finger before his face. Look closely, she advised, as close up as you dare. Can you see the place in the skin below the middle digit?

That was where the band had been at home. Look at the impression it left behind in the skin. It's like the mark of a brassiere after you remove it. Or your stockings where they have been rolled tight against the thigh.

McQuade thought, What a thing to say. Uneasy, he said, The way you talk, one would think he had taken off your stockings.

I wonder where else he touched me when he took it? she said. I wonder what else he took? I wonder how he took it off?

I don't want to hear about it, McQuade said. And you must understand, it is my fault entirely that he took the ring. Also, the two others. He told her the whole story. And how the three rings would let the five friends escape aboard the *Evergreen.*

Excited by this report, she sat up on her knees beside him and clasped her hands together in the space between her thighs. Then I have helped you to be reunited with your girl friend! she said.

Exactly! McQuade said, pleased she had grasped the heart of the matter so quickly. And you have done so much more than that. You have helped to save her life—my life, too.

And so you owe me a favor, she said.

I owe you a hundred favors! he said.

Why, then you must repay me, every one of them!

Tell me how to begin, he said.

You must reunite me with Sanderson, and save my life, too. Hold on, I have a plan. You must put me aboard the *Evergreen.*

We will take you with us then, I promise, he said. We will go on board together.

No, you misunderstand, you must put me on board first, before Sanderson and the others. Imagine how surprised he will be, believing he has left me behind, when he discovers I will be sailing at his side.

What if he doesn't want you there? McQuade ventured.

All the more reason not to give him the opportunity of saying no.

You would insist then? Even when you weren't wanted?

Ah, McQuade, I must have someone.

And so must I.

Everyone needs someone.

And you think there is only the one? he said.

Playfully, she pinched his cheek. What if your girl falls for Sanderson? she teased. What if he becomes excited by just the thought of her. Such overnight affairs are commonplace in wartime. Nothing else can touch them for the abandonment and passion of the lovers; they behave as if they haven't the time left to hug and kiss. If that happens to them, what will you do then, McQuade?

In answer, McQuade seized her hand and kissed her finger where the ring had been.

After you put me aboard, she said, nuzzling her face into his hair, I will write you a note telling my father to let you have the car. Then you can rescue Sanderson and his friends. You will have to hurry, though. You may make the dock with only seconds to spare—you may even be chased across the city by another car. You should have your boat ready, with its motor running.

She rose and, after stretching and yawning at the foot of the bed, pulled her gown over her head and threw it to the floor. Naked, she confronted her wardrobe and selected a sailor blouse and skirt from the rack. These she found fault with in the full-length mirror, twisting her hips left and right while she craned her neck to see how they looked from behind. She removed this outfit and stood naked before the mirror, pouting as she pondered what next to wear. She remembered McQuade then. You didn't like it, either, did you? she said, turning to him. So that he could see her better, she placed a large pillow behind him, propping up his head. She tried on several different costumes, turning from the mirror to McQuade and back again. Well, what do you say? she said.

I say you should keep trying until you find what you like, he said. This is a wonderful show, Mitzi. I love watching you dress and undress, your movements in and out of your clothes are more graceful than ballet.

Finally, to McQuade's disappointment, she decided on a polo shirt and linen slacks.

Remember, what we have discussed is our secret, she said; do you agree?

McQuade nodded.

But instead, he went to the naval attaché as soon as he could and told him of their plans to put Mitzi aboard the *Evergreen,* hoping he would agree to give him the car without his first having to spend the time to take Mitzi to the ship.

To his surprise, the attaché agreed to the plan, which he judged a good one. You must do as she says, he counseled. She is cleverer sometimes than we give her credit for. She would be wise to leave the country as soon as she can. At the moment a corridor is still open between the embassy and the harbor—you should have safe passage—but how long it can be kept open, no one can predict. The situation is so unclear and volatile. I must tell you that the embassy itself is no longer safe. It could be seized, hostages could be taken. Diplomatic immunity will count for nothing if that comes to pass.

McQuade played his trump card. You misunderstand, he said. She plans to meet Sanderson aboard.

The attaché lost all control of the muscles in his face; he collapsed in a chair, where he buried his face in his hands. What a fool, I should have guessed as much, he said. And I suppose your Sally will be aboard also?

McQuade, feeling guilty, nodded.

Lucky fellow then, he said. How I envy you! How I wish I could go with you aboard the *Evergreen*!

McQuade waited for Mitzi in the embassy garden. Just outside the fence, a mob had taken to marching in the street. Death to the general! it shouted, several thousand strong. Suddenly there were drifting clouds of tear gas, gunfire and many screams. McQuade went over to the gate and watched the panic of the mob as it was turned back by the tanks and the baton-swinging troops.

The ambassador himself came outdoors to assess the situation. Who knows what dictator this violence will sweep into power? he said. This poor unhappy country. The untold sufferings of humanity. Such a tragic place, our planet. He guided McQuade to a garden seat among the banana trees, where he bade him sit down beside him. He confronted McQuade with his misty eyes. Odd, isn't it, he said, how a man, even at my age, can have this overpowering desire to leave his old life behind. Imagine it, a man who simply wants to run off like the wind, leave the family, the old homestead, the old school ties, the old friends, and make a fresh start again. Yes, by heavens, a man ought to be able to make good his escape any number of times in his lifetime. Take myself, for instance. I dearly miss my wife, who is home on our little horse farm in the Cumberland Valley, and, to be sure, I love my children and have always sought the best for them. But sometimes this inconsolable urge comes over me, McQuade, and it tells me I could leave them overnight without so much as thinking twice or looking back. And never see them again either. Give them up to oblivion, as it were. Now, what do you say to that?

It sounds lonesome, McQuade said.

It is lonesome, the ambassador agreed. But it is exhilarating and liberating, too.

But you don't do it, McQuade said.

But I don't do it, the ambassador repeated, nodding in agreement. The very counsel I wanted from you, and what I have come to expect from someone like yourself. Wisely said, my young friend.

McQuade had come around to the front of the embassy where he had met Mitzi when the naval attaché came running out to catch him before he left. I have good news for you, so good it may break your heart, he said, breathlessly. Steady now. We have just learned from our informants that an American woman being held by the army and believed to be a supporter of the rebels has just escaped. Who else could she be but your Sally Sunstrum? It seems likely that she is waiting for you in the appointed place.

Dear God, did you say waiting for me? McQuade said. He went out of his head with grief and anticipation.

It seemed that Sally herself appeared before him in that moment. They met in a cornfield in a landscape that resembled Wisconsin. She came toward him down the very corn row in which he had stretched out, resting on his back. The breeze rattled the corn stalks and disturbed her frock. Sally, he cried, now that you are free, be a good girl, come home to me!

She broke off an ear of corn and shucked it in her

hands, peeling back the leaves and parting the silk to bare the tip of the cob. She said, Tonight I will sleep in a soft bed with laundered sheets and a pillow beneath my head. I won't sleep in the dirt, McQuade.

Nothing wrong with this earth, Sally, McQuade said. It's the miracle of the planet, as my father is fond of saying. It will grow anything. All it needs is the plow.

I should think you would be content to sleep alone, she said. All your life you have been interested only in yourself. As it stands now, no woman in her right mind would want to keep you company.

Come now, McQuade protested, choosing to misunderstand her, I am not so unlovable as that.

She said, You remind me of my brothers and their school friends buried in all those foreign battlefields in lands the names of which I can't pronounce. It would take a round-the-world excursion to visit all their graves. We would require a map to find their white crosses among the fields of thousands. Just today my father said, Where are all my little boys in argyle socks and knickerbockers? Hush, my mother answered, they are dead, and you know it; killed one after another in all these terrible foreign wars we have been fighting lately. I can still recall my brothers. They glued model airplanes on Saturday mornings while they listened to the radio. They raced down sidewalks in their red wagons. I should imagine they accepted their lonely destinies with dignity, knowing they had done their duty by their friends. So long for now, McQuade. Who can understand young men?

She stepped over him and continued on her way. What can I do now that you are permanently ashore in some unpronounceable port of call, she called back over her shoulder, except give myself completely to some other cause?

As soon as McQuade returned to his senses, he took Mitzi by the hand and ran down the palm-lined boulevards that comprised the corridor to the sea. This was kept open by a thin line of government troops augmented by a battalion of American paratroopers in battle gear who had been brought into the airport before the runways were in range of the enemy guns. They waved McQuade and Mitzi past their checkpoints, signaling them to hurry. McQuade hoped the gunfire he heard ahead of them was just the nervous firing of a few unruly troops.

They took a shortcut down back alleys that were the homes of strip joints, tattoo parlors and small casinos. They came to the warehouses and the crowded waterfront section inhabited by the Chinese, where they made their way through a traffic jam of bicycles, hand-drawn carts and herds of milling goats. So many Chinese were running in and out of their doorways, carrying children and bundles, preparing to flee. If the rebels take the city, a man warned them, the gunboats in the harbor will turn their cannon on the city. They will blow everybody up, friend and foe alike.

At the docks, the fleet of fishing boats and the

many small untidy sailboats that hauled freight were packed together in a crowd of masts and cabins. One could walk for blocks, it seemed, stepping only on the decks of boats. The boatmen were on board their boats, waiting to take on passengers. McQuade ran up and down the dock, trying to strike a bargain, while Mitzi followed behind, pleading. But the boatmen were waiting to take aboard the government big shots and generals who planned to flee at the last minute with their families and jewels, and who would pay money, big money. Some said they would not go out into the harbor anytime soon, not for love nor money. The navy patrol boats were firing on any small craft they suspected of ferrying deserters or rebel ammunition. Sometimes they simply used these boats as target practice for their gunners. McQuade could hear cannon and the stutter of machine guns coming off the water. To Mitzi, he whispered, We will have to steal a boat.

Crouching behind the many crates of coffee beans and green bananas, they watched the string of boats. When the owner of a small rowboat came onto the dock to confer with a businessman who was showing him the several colors of his paper money, McQuade said to Mitzi, Quickly! Now is our best chance! Making certain they were hidden behind the crates, they made their way across the dock; then they made a mad dash across the open area and down the float, leaping into the empty boat. Mitzi leaned out over the bow and untied the rope from the piling as McQuade, at the oars, rowed with all his failing strength. When they were free of the tangle of other boats and into the open water, they could see the boat owner on the dock, shouting at them and making threatening gestures that composed a kind of war dance. Meanwhile, the city enlarged behind them, roofs and chimneys silhouetted against the orange sky.

They rowed silently past the anchored freighters whose foreign crews were hanging over the rails and spitting into the oily water.

Hey, you, mate! they called. Ahoy there, over here! Both of you!

Why? Mitzi said.

Never mind why, the sailors said. We will show you when you get here.

What do you have? Mitzi asked.

Come and see, the sailors said.

But McQuade ignored them and kept to his oars. They drifted into the shadow of a gunboat, gray-colored, with a high streamlined hull that hovered above them menacingly. The decks were bristling with cannon.

Then McQuade made out the *Evergreen.* Over near the mouth of the harbor. A white hull and a red cross on its smokestack. He had no sooner set his course for it than he entered the field of the battle that was taking place. The sea, choppy now that he was clear of the channel, splashed up around them with explosions and the shrapnel of the falling shells. Puffs of smoke drifted on the breeze. Speedboats played hide-and-seek behind the anchored ships, emerging to drop torpedoes that misfired and exploded harmlessly of their own accord, making fountains of spray and water. The old Spanish fortress on the island in the harbor answered with its heavy guns.

A large motor launch with an open cockpit appeared out of the smoke and splash, speeding toward the city. Just as it was about to pass on McQuade's starboard, a salvo landed before its bow, sending up a tremendous waterspout, and the boat, to avoid it, suddenly veered to port, throwing up a wall of water that left McQuade's boat rocking precariously in its wake. But the launch had come close enough for McQuade to have made out the name of its mother ship and the logos of the pine tree on its bow. It was the launch from the *Evergreen*! And within hailing distance, with its engine cut and bobbing in the wash. McQuade, standing and waving, recognized several of his shipmates. And the chief engineer himself on board and shouting at the rowboat through a megaphone. Is that you, McQuade? he called. You damn young pup, we were headed for shore to find you. We had just about given up trying to run that cross fire when we said let's give it one more try, for the sake of our shipmate. We didn't want to leave without you—don't protest—you would have done the same for us. At least you have had the good sense to return by yourself. But look here, my lovely, you can't expect to bring a girl on board!

The sailors on the launch laughed.

This response gave McQuade reason to pause. What had made him assume that Captain Lundholm of the *Evergreen* would be willing to take his friends aboard his ship? He might deny them passage, might turn them away, cut their boat adrift. It might be steamship company policy not to carry passengers, or a violation of international maritime law to take refugees aboard. Their plan to escape could come to nothing in the last moment. He had been rash to promise such a sanctuary to his friends.

Standing up in his boat, McQuade shouted, Come alongside! Take us into your launch. My passenger is the daughter of the American ambassador. You have orders to take her on board the *Evergreen.*

So long as you are coming with her, the chief replied. None of your tricks now, my boy.

The two craft drifted close; the sailors caught McQuade's gunwhales and steadied both boats as Mitzi stepped into the launch.

When it was the turn of McQuade, he was sorely tempted. He had no desire to return to so dangerous a city, and there were worse fates than remaining in the company of the lovely Mitzi, who had already shown that she could become the object of his powerful desires; they might share a cabin on the *Evergreen* and stroll the promenade deck, arm in arm. But instead of yielding to these impulses, he pushed himself away and took to his oars in a flurry of strokes that tore at his shoulders and ribs. I promised to return this boat to its owner! he called to his dumbfounded shipmates. I'll return as soon as I can!

You damn fool! the chief shouted after him through his megaphone. How can you possibly return if you give up the boat? He gave orders to the seaman at the wheel to give chase. But the seaman had trouble re-starting the engine, which gave McQuade the time he needed to pull away.

When McQuade reached that stretch of water where the shells were landing in a cross fire, he hid behind a freighter that had received a hit; a small fire was burning on her deck, which the African sailors were dousing with firehoses while a column of black smoke obscured the air. Finally the launch from the *Evergreen* was under way, its bow cutting the water into a v-shape as it came after McQuade. But when it, too, entered the battle zone, it came about quickly and retreated at full throttle for the safety of the mother ship. While McQuade watched helplessly, the launch shot up suddenly in the water as if it had struck a submerged object or had been lifted by a giant wave. Just before it drifted behind an oil tanker, where it was out of sight, it had appeared to capsize in an explosion of smoke and spray.

As McQuade began to make his way on foot across the city to the embassy, he met his mother on a street corner where she had stationed herself to meet him. She wore her nurse's uniform, including the blue cape, and the white cap with the red cross on its face. No one else was on the street, not even soldiers.

McQuade said, I'm a bit exhausted, Mother, from all the excitement and rowing. I'm not sure I can reach the embassy without your aid.

She stood beside an ambulance. It was gray and

long like a hearse, with its rear doors open. The driver was his father. Dressed in his doorman's uniform of the downtown Milwaukee hotel, he looked like a field marshal. He helped his wife wrap McQuade's head in a bandage, leaving only two holes for his eyes. Then they put his left arm in a sling. This is your disguise, his mother said. They placed him on a stretcher and guided him into the ambulance; his mother rode with him in the back while his father took the wheel, racing them across the city. They passed through gunfire and clouds of tear gas. Civilians were lying facedown in the street, hugging the pavement. At the barricades, his father had only to point to the nurse in the rear comforting the wounded man on the stretcher, and the soldiers, after peering in, would salute and wave them through. Again the sky was orange, the earth black. An orange sky above the jumble of the black rooftops of the city. McQuade didn't imagine that.

If you had settled down and married, his mother said, no harm would have come to you. Now it is too late to save yourself in a woman's face. Or in the merciful power of her love. Too late to perpetuate yourself in children. A fatal mistake, my son, was made in visiting a foreign port of call. But you are doing the right thing at last by returning to the right beginning for your proper ending. Of all earthly hiding places, there is no better place than this.

Comfort me along the way, McQuade mumbled.

She said, Do you remember the lullabies I used to sing you when you wouldn't go to sleep because of all the bears dancing in the dark around your bed?

I am not recalling them, he said.

She took him in her arms, reciting, The wind has blown, the rope has broken, the cradle has fallen, down comes my baby boy. . . .

What is that you are saying? McQuade said, trying to raise his head. What kind of a rhyme is that to tell a child?

The ambulance pulled into the courtyard of the embassy.

This is as far as I can go, his mother said. Hereafter you are on your own. Seek asylum in the embassy. The ambassador is sympathetic. He won't let the intrigue and violence of the other side violate these gates.

The embassy is a fine place, McQuade said. But, if it is all the same to you, I would just as soon go home.

So it was on the first day of school, she said. You cried that day, too, how you cried. But you stuck it out, you little man, and you didn't cry again.

Mother, he called after her. Before you go, please tell me what is happening, if you know. It's not as if I am asking why.

Perhaps we are all a dream of death, she said. And you cannot go beyond the people and the places of this dream. You are inside yourself and never again to be outside yourself. The dream is all you have left of life itself.

Hearing this, McQuade couldn't help himself, he burst into tears.

Make your reconciliations with what you know has been your life, she said, and with all of us who knew you when. Make them, as only you can, within the dream. Now, dry those tears. Chin up. Shoulder high. Turn yourself around, go forth and don't look back. Remember, always wear your sweater in a draft. Bundle up in your wraps if you go outdoors into the cold. Keep your feet warm. Also, dry. And don't bolt down your dinner. The last one from the table shall be the last one to the grave.

Once more Fortune awaited execution. This time as he was temporarily imprisoned in one of the cadet cells of the old military academy. His heavy door, with its barred window, opened onto the parade grounds surrounded by a high wall, against the south side of which many of the army's prisoners—the suspected terrorists, fifth columnists and deserters—were being shot before the army was forced to withdraw from this quarter of the city.

He had been picked up by a patrol only a block away from Gabriella's apartment. He had been unable to talk his way out this predicament, and the soldiers had run him down and overpowered him easily when he made a halfhearted attempt at escape. He had been surprised at how little fight was left inside him; he had as good as walked into the enemy's hands. He had become weak and reckless. And resigned, besides. He was like that fellow McQuade. Nor was his luck any better than McQuade's.

As he had been marched off to his makeshift prison, he had caught sight of as many as a dozen bodies on the pavement a block away. Even at that distance he was afraid he had recognized Gabriella among them—had made out the khaki blouse, the dark hair, a brown arm, so slender at the wrist. He could not be certain, of course, and his captors would not allow him to investigate. It was just as well. To have identified her would have been to abandon hope. From that moment, he wandered in a daze, unable to care about himself. Hereafter, it would not be otherwise.

And who should turn out to be in command of the troops who had detained him but the infamous Major Hilario himself, who had recognized him a second time. This time, you pig, he said, you will not escape God's punishment. Bang, bang, and you will go right to hell, you gringo.

The major was like a knife, Fortune thought, listening to him rant and rave. His intelligence, heart, even his penis were probably knife-shaped. He imagined the man's head like a knife and his using it to slit the soft underbelly of a giant fish. Fortune no longer had the strength or will to fight against that knife.

The next he knew, he was seated on the stone floor in a corner of the cadet's cell. A young air force captain amused himself by keeping him company until it was his turn to be dragged out and stood against the wall. The captain was blond and was outfitted immaculately in a sand-colored uniform with highly polished boots and silver wings across his breast. A pilot, he had been drafted to help out the army during the siege of the city once the airport had fallen and he could no longer reach his plane. He was in the mood for a little conversation and was disappointed that thus far Fortune had refused to talk.

Fortune had laid out his wrinkled snapshots of Gabriella side by side on the floor. They had been taken all over Latin America and showed her in various costumes and poses. There she was in jungle khaki; now in a bathing suit at a beach; here in a peasant blouse at an outdoor café.

Are you playing solitaire? the captain asked, observing him.

No, the opposite, Fortune said.

How worn down and indifferent Fortune felt. All those hard times and close scrapes were taking their toll. The many arduous journeys down those unhealthy jungle rivers, the parachute jumps behind the enemy lines. The bluffs and bribes. All those unscrupulous dealings with unsavory characters. I have something to tell you, Captain, he said, weakly.

The captain, who had all but given up on the idea of a conversation, perked up. He came over and stooped down. I am listening, he said.

I am not so innocent, Fortune said.

I know that, replied the captain. You are a great sinner.

I never murdered, raped or pillaged, Fortune said.

You never heard me say you did, the captain replied. But surely you cheated, lied and were generally disreputable and sneaky. Do you have a last request?

Fortune managed a smile. Tell me you have heard from the governor, he said

All right, you silly fellow, the captain said, we have heard from the governor.

And what did he say?

What did you want him to say?

That I am pardoned, Fortune said.

Very well, the captain said, laughing, you have been pardoned.

You say this only to torment me, Fortune said. How do I know you are telling the truth?

Because, as I told you, it was contained in a message that came from the governor, he said. It said, Please pardon the American criminal. How is that?

What I wanted to hear.

Of course, you know it has come too late to make a difference, he said. You are already as good as dead.

I know, I know, Fortune said, sighing. Still, it is something to be pardoned, all the same.

The captain withdrew across the room and gazed out at the parade ground through the bars. He said, right now, I confess I feel for you as I would for a woman I once loved passionately but to whom I am now indifferent. However, I am on your side entirely in this matter of your execution. To me it is an inexcusable cruelty. Killing you in cold blood—he shuddered—it is like making love to a whore. Oh, I can understand killing in a passion, it is like making love to your young mistress with whom you are infatuated—hopelessly so. There is so little passion these days and so much torturing and killing. I am sure your executioners feel toward you exactly the indifference I myself am feeling. One would think indifference would lead to passivity, nonchalance, inaction. I don't understand how one can inflict pain and death when one is cold, objective, detached. Surely it must follow that one cannot give pleasure—cannot give love and affection—at such an hour? How is it that one can deal out cruelty and pain?

Fortune filled up his mind with images of Gabriella. Long ago she would have returned safely to the apartment; by now she and the others would have been put safely aboard McQuade's ship, which would have been quick to raise anchor and leave the port. He imagined the ship putting in at a harbor in the neighboring state, and Gabriella finding sanctuary ashore. She would be shopping in a market for fresh fruit, her string bag hanging from her arm; or maybe taking coffee beneath an umbrella in an outdoor café. He saw her in sunlight, wearing sandals and sunglasses. With several glinting bracelets along her arm.

And McQuade's girl also safe, and to think that he, Fortune, had contributed to her rescue! To the reuniting of the young lovers.

He laughed, saying to himself, They will be sorry in the morning when they learn that I have been pardoned and in the next breath that I am dead.

It amused him to concentrate on what he planned to shout when they made him stand against that blasted wall with its scree of brick dust against the base as though it had been knocked out by a pickax instead of bullets. Gabriella! he would shout. She would hear him even if she was at sea on the decks of the *Evergreen;* even as far away as the boulevards of the capital of the neighboring republic. She would be stopped in her tracks and turn about, so powerful would be the ringing of his voice. She would hear him call even if she was among the heap of bodies in the street. Even then she would lift her head.

Just before the firing squad let loose with their deadly volley, he would shout, *Viva el amor!*

McQuade had no sooner returned safely to the embassy than Mr. Swanson, the chief engineer of the *Evergreen,* made an appearance. He was in his dress uniform and held his hat tucked under his arm. He stood among his escort of sailors like a great circus bear, coughing into his fist and shuffling his feet. Your excellency, he kept repeating.

I understand my daughter is aboard your ship, the ambassador said, helping him out.

Well, yes, that was her intention, the engineer stammered. And ours, also, I may add—to have her there, I mean. This is the matter I have come about. The captain would have come himself; in my judgment it was his duty to have done so, however . . .

I appreciate your doing what you can for her, the ambassador interrupted, kindly. I know only too well how headstrong and troublesome she can be.

Do what we can for her? the chief repeated. Ah, that's just it, what can anyone do for her?

You have her exactly! the ambassador said, admiringly. She will have a hard time putting one over on the likes of you!

The chief engineer looked uncomfortable. He glanced toward the naval attaché for help.

Go ahead, deliver your message, the attaché said.

Your excellency, the chief began, I am an uneducated man, born of common Kentucky people, familiar with slag heaps and hollows. When I first went to sea, I shipped out as a coal passer. After a while I earned a fireman's and an oiler's ticket, and finally worked my way up to the officer's rank of engineer. My world is the firehole, sir. I know about valves, boilers, furnaces, the ship's screw. Steam, fire and smoke comprise my atmosphere, so forgive me if I confine myself to those terms.

The escort of sailors grew restless and searched about the room, as though seeking an avenue of escape.

You see, sir, the chief continued, down in the firehole the coal passers shovel coal into the furnaces; the fire from the coal boils the water to make the steam; steam turns the pistons; the pistons turn the screw; the screw propels the ship. As everyone must know, burned-out coal is reduced to ashes. These ashes are no longer capable of producing power—no longer useful for anything, as far as I can see. He did his best to go on at this point but became too tongue-tied to speak. He mopped his brow. What I mean, he was saying, about down below and such . . .

The naval attaché was exasperated. He said, What is this drivel you insist on talking? The city is blowing up in our faces, we may have to escape at any moment, his excellency can't stand here forever listening to such drivel.

The ambassador smiled. He said, not unkindly, Please continue, Chief Engineer.

What I mean to say is this, the chief said. Some pieces burn in a nice red glow and produce a marvelous heat. They are what I would call first-rate lumps of coal. They'll burn longer than the others, too. So many of the others will burn out right away. He looked at the ambassador expectantly. He said, Does that suggest something to your excellency?

The ambassador shook his head.

The chief was disappointed. He said, What good are they, you might ask, and it would be a good question, too! Once more he paused, waiting for some response.

Well? the ambassador said at last.

Perhaps these coals are like men, the chief said. Adding, And like women, too. Even young women—who are close to you and mean a lot to you!

The ambassador said, If you say so. He looked amused, but his face was pale. Two lines of perspiration showed upon his face, one along his forehead and the other above his lip.

Come to the point! the naval attaché demanded.

The chief took a deep breath. As you may have heard, he reported, young McQuade here put your daughter aboard our launch as we were making our way across the harbor.

McQuade confirmed this. It's true, he said. I did as he says.

We were taking heavy fire as we attempted to return to the mother ship, the chief said.

This is also true, McQuade said. I was a witness.

A shell landed just off our bow, the chief said, and the launch was overturned by the shock and splash. All hands went into the sea and were saved. But your beautiful daughter, unlike the rest of us, hadn't a life jacket—she was overboard before she had the chance to put one on her shoulders. We searched but couldn't find her in the water. Her body has still to be recovered, but, take my word for it, she must have perished. Abandon any hope that she remains alive! You must forgive me, if you can!

The ambassador did not hesitate to embrace the weeping chief engineer. He said, Good Chief Engineer, of course I forgive you. I have no doubts that, as a responsible seaman, you did your duty. And it was a heroic service you performed just now. To himself, he mumbled, You were like those messengers in the tragedies of old.

The naval attaché stood with his head bowed, his face covered by his hands. He eased himself backward to a couch where he reclined, writhing and weeping before suddenly lying very still with an arm thrown across his eyes.

The ambassador felt behind him for a chair and, as though he were afraid he might fall, sat down. Ah, well, these things happen, he said. Life goes on, that sort of thing. Who knows what awful fate might have been in store for her tomorrow, or two years hence, had she lived to see that day. But he wept all the same. He asked for a cigarette, and one of the sailors obliged him, shaking out a smoke. I don't normally smoke, the ambassador explained.

Unable to take the intensity of so unhappy a scene, McQuade escaped into the garden. How ironic, he thought, that poor Mitzi in her attempt to rendezvous with Sanderson had failed to reach the *Evergreen,* whereas he, against all odds, had returned safely to the embassy. His own good fortune, however, was also his guilt. But for the present, there was little he could do about that. In the meantime he would be safe inside the embassy. Safer, certainly, than elsewhere hereabouts. It was not improbable that eventually he would leave this country on his own two feet and live elsewhere to a ripe old age. He would have been content to stay put and await this happening, if it were not for Sally. How could he forget his Sally! Come, McQuade, he urged, rouse yourself and save your friends! Once more onto the embattled streets, braving the risk of capture and torture. Death, even. There is no time to waste! All the same he doubted if he had the strength or courage to leave the sanctuary of the embassy, or to survive it if he did. Fortunately, he could afford to rest awhile. After all, both Sanderson and Fortune were out there in his place, working on his behalf. They were not merely surrogates, either, but almost, in a sense, men like himself. Except that they would be doubly effective, two heads being better than one.

* * *

In Gabriella's apartment, Sanderson maintained his vigil at Sally's bed. Her fever felt dangerous beneath his palm. While he nursed her, she faded in and out of sleep, sometimes into so deep a sleep he feared she had lapsed into a coma. She must have quinine, he said.

When to his great relief he saw her eyes open, he said, It's Sanderson, I was with you in the mountains, do you remember?

Poor McQuade, was all she said.

Poor yourself, thought Sanderson, so moved he had to turn away.

Please look at me, McQuade, she said.

She was delirious, he told himself; what else explained this response? He leaned above her and stared into her face. Her eyes were wide and searching, but he wondered if they could see. Again she called him McQuade.

Here I am, he said. But why do you call me poor McQuade?

Ah, a smile crossed her face; that was a good sign. I was remembering that winter night you hitchhiked to my college, she said in a small voice barely above a whisper. You stood beneath my window, shivering.

Until you took pity on me, Sanderson said.

That was not pity I was feeling, she said.

This will break my heart, Sanderson said to himself.

Once again he went to the window and tried to determine the present line of the rebels' advance. He reckoned they were as close as a dozen blocks. It would be the end for them if they were still here when the rebels broke through. On the other hand, he could not risk exposing Sally on the street while the army, from which she had just escaped, was still in control. Their escape, he realized, depended solely on McQuade. What on earth was keeping the man? Fortune was right; he should not have trusted McQuade.

Once again he remembered those three rings; they could explain McQuade's absence. The ambassador had discovered the theft, placed the blame in the proper quarter and was not about, in these terrible times, to hand over a car to save the thief.

In his despair, Sanderson wished now he had gone with McQuade. In the embassy he would be reasonably safe. Understandably, he might be in trouble because of the rings, but he would have explained his actions and promised to make restitution. Instead, he had followed Gabriella onto Smoke Street. Now here he was, nursing McQuade's girl friend and waiting for the end. His acts of friendship would be the death of him!

Frustrated by his helplessness, he ran out into the street to look for help. To his surprise, an old-fashioned taxi was parked at the curb, the only vehicle on the street. A peroxide blonde, the mistress of an army officer, was loading up the taxi with her belongings. Already she had filled the backseat with her furs. Next to us, Sanderson thought, she must be the last to leave.

Will you take myself and a friend with you? Sanderson asked the driver.

The driver rubbed his thumb and index finger together to mean it costs money, much money.

I have something better than money, Sanderson said, and produced the ring that Fortune had returned to him. You can have it in exchange for a ride to the American Embassy.

The driver had an unshaven chin but no hair on his cheeks. He refused the ring. How do I know if it is a real jewel in there? he said. I am not a jeweler. A man like me has to have cash. Again he made the gesture with his fingers, meaning money.

The woman was taking a long time to load the taxi, which made the driver nervous. She carried out a caged parakeet and a pet chihuahua, and pushed them into the back with the furs.

I will help you if I can, she said to Sanderson. Take your ring to the pawnbroker in the building across the street—if he is still there. If he buys it, come back here with the money, and maybe the driver will take you and your friend away from here. In a whisper, she said, I will try to keep him here as long as I can.

Against all expectations, Sanderson found the pawnbroker inside his shop, but with two valises packed and ready to depart at any moment. Of course, Sanderson thought, at such a time as the present, with so many of the middle class eager to exchange their treasures for the cash required to leave the country, he would stay in business until the last possible minute; it was the best of a buyer's market.

The pawnbroker was an old man who wore a skullcap and bedroom slippers. You are my last customer, he announced. Quickly, show me what you have.

Confidently, Sanderson produced the ring. The pawnbroker smiled and weighed it in his ancient hand. He took it into his cage, where he fit his jeweler's glass into his eye and examined it beneath a light. Such exquisite workmanship, he pronounced. A perfectly cut stone, a handsome setting. A superior ring in all respects.

Pay me enough to hire a taxi, Sanderson said, and the ring is yours.

You would sell as cheaply as that? the pawnbroker wondered. But even at that price, you would pay too dearly. May I ask how you came by such a ring? Because it is not a man's ring. And facetiously, to prove his point, he attempted to slide the band around Sanderson's small finger. See, it doesn't even fit the littlest one, he said. No, I should say it belonged to a young woman—someone who was vivacious, impulsive, possessive.

Never mind how I came by that ring, Sanderson ordered. Or whose hand it fits.

But I must mind, insisted the pawnbroker. And I shall mind. What if you hacked a finger off a corpse in order to steal this ring? And when Sanderson started to protest, he said, Oh, so you do admit you removed it from a living woman, I think that is even worse. Look at you. Don't you think a man of my experience can tell the physical signs of guilt? The perspiration on the brow, the trembling hands. And I must say I am surprised at your criminal behavior. Obviously, you are educated, affluent, nice to look at. You have had all the advantages. A good life—or a good start in life—in other words. Take the advice of an old man who has seen the sadness and tragedy of the world come to his doorstep from its four corners, and who has little enough time left on this earth himself, and return the ring. Sure, it is only a ring the first time out. But next time, it will be a newsstand, a candy store, perhaps in the end you will knock over a bank. You are a young fellow with a long lifetime ahead of you, you wouldn't want a little crime like the theft of this ring to be a black mark against you all your life?

All my life? Sanderson said, incredulous. It will cost me my life if I don't sell you that ring!

Just as the police have a book listing all the stolen articles, the pawnbroker said, the Lord, our God, also has a book for fallen men. And once your name is in it . . .

A philosopher! Sanderson said, wanting to choke him. I ask you again, take the ring for the price of a cab!

And deprive you of your opportunity to redeem yourself? he said. Not on your life. Return the ring to the young lady who owns it. Or to her family, if she is dead. No one will be the wiser. If you are discovered in your attempt to make restitution, throw yourself upon the mercy of your victims and of those higher powers that will judge you. It is all you can hope for. You have placed in my hands the power of your redemption. Here he handed back the ring. Now I am returning it where it belongs, he said. And, if I am any judge of character, it is in good hands, too.

* * *

Sanderson decided he would hurry on foot to Seafarers, since it was closer than the embassy. De Groot and Pendleton could be counted on to provide him with help. They would know what to do, whom to contact. Yes, he assured himself, this was the wisest course of action under the circumstances.

To his surprise the streets were almost empty. The few soldiers he encountered were uninterested in his presence. They peered warily from behind the corners of buildings or knelt behind makeshift barricades in the street. Civilians were surprised huddled in the doorways as though taking shelter from a sudden downpour.

He found the office of Ramirez and Koppleman, Seafarers, Limited, ransacked and deserted. Obviously de Groot and Pendleton had either fled in a hurry or been arrested. Sanderson supposed that the two men themselves could have created the disorder in their haste to gather their possessions and destroy the evidence. It seemed more likely, however, that the police had taken the place apart in their search for contraband and incriminating documents.

Sanderson decided that he had best set out for the embassy on his own, even though such a course would remove him farther yet from the stricken Sally. The battle for the city sounded as though it must have moved into the midtown section of Smoke Street.

The closer he drew to the embassy, the more choked the boulevards and alleyways became with people. They poured out of the buildings and side streets. Entire families were in flight, carrying bundles and suitcases. Sanderson guessed they must be making for the airport or harbor, either one.

On the contrary, their destination was the same as his. When he turned the corner, he saw the huge crowd gathering in the streets outside the embassy. It made him think of India. The forefront of the crowd pushed against the gates, while many of the younger men attempted to scale the walls. So many had their hands in the air, waving passports. Some only sought the international sanctuary of the embassy grounds, while others hoped to receive immigration visas to the United States. He caught himself thinking, There is no helping Sally; I have done all I can for her; I must save myself. He tried to push his way through the crush that impeded him, repeating, I am an American, you must let me through. But no one made way for him. Who did he think he was? He could identify himself if only he could get within earshot of the marine guards at the gate. But he soon abandoned this effort as too dangerous. He might be trampled or suffocated in the pushing horde. Certainly he would be trapped if he did not beat a retreat while he still had the chance. Already the refugees had accumulated behind him, many deep, and were pressing him forward. But just before he made good his escape, while he was jumping up and down to better see above the heads in front, he had observed the embassy flag flying at half-mast. Who could that be for? he wondered, full of dread.

* * *

On his way back to Gabriella's, Sanderson ran into an army lieutenant, his own age, in paratrooper camouflage. He drew his pistol from his holster and made Sanderson stand against the wall while he felt his clothes for weapons. Down the block a contingent of the lieutenant's soldiers were beating looters, both men and boys.

No messages on you either, the lieutenant said. You are not a courier?

I am an American, Sanderson explained.

An American on Smoke Street, the lieutenant said, amused, don't make me laugh. How could you be so lost?

Set me free and you will not see my face again, I promise, Sanderson offered.

You are right, I won't see it again, the lieutenant said; nor will anyone else, if you continue in the direction you are walking. Haven't you seen how you are the only one going forward while all the others, including the soldiers, are pulling back? In no time the legions of the notorious General Faustino will be overrunning this very piece of pavement on which you and I are standing. When those fellows come rushing through, they will blow away everyone in their path. God, how they loathe foreigners, they are pitiless with Americans. And they do not differentiate between a man and a woman, it is all the same throat to them. By the way, if you are lucky, they will only cut your throat. They have a fascination for beheading prisoners, it is a habit from the guerrilla days in the bush when bullets were worth more than lives. Believe me, their swords are dull from so many years of cutting sugarcane. To save you from such an ignominious fate, I should have you shot. If I see you on these streets again, I will shoot you myself.

Interpreting this as a dismissal, Sanderson began to edge away.

Maybe I will decide to shoot you in the back, the lieutenant called after him. I am trying to make up my mind. If you continue in that direction despite my warning, I would be doing you a big favor.

Sanderson braced himself for the worst.

Maybe I will only wing you! the lieutenant shouted.

Fortunately, by this time, Sanderson had safely turned the corner.

At Gabriella's place, Sanderson was afraid the rebel troops kicking in the doors of the shops at the end of the street had seen him enter the building. He hurried inside and found Sally no better. If anything, she was worse. She was still delirious and feverish, and all color had vanished from her face. It did not seem possible that she could travel. With horror, Sanderson remembered the vial of poison he had left on the windowsill. Just the sight of it sickened him. As if to remove it from his thoughts, he put it in his pocket. He went to the window. The rebels were swarming in the strange park across the way; already they had set up camp in the shadow of that overgrown mound of building stone or bedrock. They appeared to be dragging things about in the dust. He wondered if they were killing people over there and using the excavation site as a mass grave for their victims. The noisy monkeys that had made the jungle vines seem windblown with their travels had become silent and inactive. Sanderson could sense, however, that they were watching.

Sally stirred and made a sound. She opened her eyes. Dearest McQuade, she said.

There it was, he was to be mistaken for McQuade again. Odd, how he had begun to imitate McQuade in these final hours. It had been an act of recklessness and impulsiveness to have gone to the Seafarers and then on to the embassy, only to return here. Perhaps he had not merely taken McQuade's place but, by some inexplicable transformation, had actually become McQuade. Think of it, no longer Sanderson, but McQuade! A merchant seaman from a prairie state. And in love with Sally. And why shouldn't he be in love with Sally? He put his arm behind her, lifting her head. He placed his cheek against her own, then kissed her on the mouth. He had never felt more tender, nor more inconsolable with longing. Dearest love, he whispered, fingering her hair, I have replaced McQuade, I am as much as McQuade, and I am more than McQuade.

Carefully he disengaged himself and returned to the window for one final look. Rebel soldiers were in the street below and scanning the windows of the building. They reminded him of peasants pointing out an animal they had treed.

Do you remember our snowball fights? Sally asked.

He turned, surprised by her voice. Every one of them, he answered.

I remember us in a garden, she said. We strolled between the borders of verbena.

Phlox and verbena, Sanderson corrected. From that moment on, my favorite flowers!

That was the day I told you what I wanted most from life, she said.

I remember, he said. You listed them. A good man, healthy children, a pony to pull a painted cart, a vegetable garden, a flower patch, a goat to milk . . .

And an evening in Prairie du Chien, she asked, what does that recall?

The first time I made love to you, Sanderson said.

She said, Poor you. You went searching for experience and adventure, but what did you find?

Love, he said.

What else?

Death, he said.

I found them, too, she said.

Then we have found everything, he said.

She made a final effort to speak.

Hush now, he cooed. You are my adventure, you have become the story of my life. As he spoke, he eased the vial from his pocket and tugged out the tiny cork with his teeth. He thought of a piece of Etruscan statuary in that moment: a man and wife shown as contented in death as they had been in life, smiling and embracing in the stone effigy atop their tomb.

* * *

McQuade found himself still wandering about the banana plantations of the embassy garden when Sally appeared before him like the vision of an angel. She wore a wedding gown.

Sally! he cried. I'm a bit dizzy from having a few drinks with the boys, forgive me for being late. Hold on, I recollect the schedule now. The wedding in the little Lutheran church in Fond du Lac. Also, the party we planned in the tavern afterwards.

You left me at the altar, she answered. For hours you couldn't hear a sound in the church for my weeping. At last the pastor blew out the candles, poured back the wine. The guitars and mandolins never strummed the happy tunes. The old women in babushkas never had a reason to dry their eyes. The drunken wedding guests never laid their plans to steal my shoe. And I never danced with you, McQuade.

We will be married, McQuade insisted. For the first time, or for the hundredth. As soon as I return from this foreign port of call.

I will come to you before you come to me, she said, her voice and image fading. But answer me this, McQuade. Why the orange sameness of our sky? Why is there neither sunset nor sundown? Who bet our moon and lost it? Who ate the stars?

The chief engineer was still at the embassy. So was the contingent of sailors from the *Evergreen.* They came out and stood beside McQuade in the garden, where they found him kneeling as though in prayer.

You have a dreadful wound, the chief pronounced. Strange that no one has noticed it. You didn't know that you were wounded?

It would explain my weakness, McQuade said, wouldn't it?

Just so, the chief agreed. All the more reason to return immediately to the *Evergreen.* The corridor to the harbor can't be kept open for much longer, and we won't sail home unless we count you among the crew.

I can't leave without my friends, McQuade said.

And what friends are these? the chief inquired.

He named his friends: Sanderson, Sally, Fortune, Gabriella.

You won't go unless they are aboard?

McQuade shook his head.

Why, then they are aboard, the chief said. Don't tell me you didn't know? Yes, aboard, you lucky fellow, and wondering at this very moment why you haven't joined them for a stroll about the deck.

McQuade kissed the chief's hand.

Yes, they made it there on their own, the chief said. While you were dillydallying here with your wound. They were not to be denied—not them!

McQuade recalled nothing of the trip across the town and harbor except that a ragged band of merchant seamen of several colors and nationalities, recruited from the ships in port and bearing sidearms, were helping to keep the corridor open to the harbor. The next he knew, his shipmates were helping him to board the *Evergreen.*

Sally! he cried. I am here! I am safe! And he staggered like a blind man about the deck, barefoot and with his arms outstretched and groping.

Get him below, said the chief engineer, and, for God's sake, do so quickly.

Such a pitiful sight, a sailor said.

Who is Sally? asked another. I don't know of any Sally on board.

Hush, man, said the chief. Mind your business.

McQuade struggled with his shipmates and kept shouting for his Sally, no matter how they tried to quiet him and hold him still.

Get him below, the chief repeated. Do as I say, and say nothing of this yourselves.

The commotion brought out the captain, who had been shut up drinking in his cabin. He came on deck, slipping on his jacket, brushing back his yellow hair. There better not be any Sally on board, he said. I will not countenance a woman on my ship.

And my good friend, Sanderson, where is he? McQuade demanded.

I don't know who you mean, the sailor said.

And no Sally either? wailed McQuade.

The chief was moved. You shall see what you shall see, was all he said.

And no Fortune, McQuade added. And no Gabriella.

The captain grasped the situation, which had the effect of sobering him quickly. You have so dangerous a fever, he explained, that we had to get you aboard at any cost. It must be a rare tropical malady you picked up when we put in at Java.

Fiji, the chief corrected.

Wherever, said the captain. Ever since that visit, you have been performing on will alone.

Then my friends are still ashore! McQuade cried, having reached this sad conclusion.

What a pitiful sight he made, struggling with his shipmates. He thrashed about until his shirt was torn. And such howls of grief that came from his lips, they would reduce strong men to tears.

Calm yourself, the captain said. You were the only one to make it home. Think what a lucky fellow you are!

Think how helpless I am, McQuade retorted. And how guilty, too.

It seemed to McQuade he must have broken loose and gotten as far as the rail, where it was his intention to dive overboard and swim ashore. But whether he actually made that dive or fell into the hold because some careless sailor had failed to close a hatch cover, he remembered only that he fell, and was still falling when he saw his brain explode with light.

He came to in a bunk in one of the officers' staterooms. He felt as though every bone in his body had been broken. Captain Lundholm himself was on hand to keep him company. McQuade could make out his heavy sandy eyebrows, the wind-beaten face, the gold stripes on his sleeve. He could see him in that orange light flooding through the open porthole. He must have stirred and moaned, because the captain stroked his arm and said, There, there, sailor, don't try to talk.

McQuade said, Where are we now, Captain?

In the same godforsaken place we were before, the captain answered. If you can tell anything by the look of the shore.

McQuade said, I had often dreamed of someday calling at a foreign port.

The captain said, It is not so foreign, McQuade. If you had traveled as much as I have, the globe becomes about as big as a kitchen garden. And the life of a sailor is just more of the same boats in the bathtub. He leaned back against the bulkhead, biting his thumbnail, frowning, rocking with the gentle creaking of the ship. At last he sighed and said, I suppose you would like to see your mother and father at such a time.

McQuade didn't know what was meant by this. He had not the strength, however, to hold back the tears.

Observing this response, the captain was quick to say, You will pull through, McQuade, you will lick the odds. As soon as this bloody sun goes up or down, as soon as we see a sunrise or sundown, as soon as that infernal orange cast to the sky gives way to black or blue, we will sail out of this port on a northward course. Who wants the stagnancy and swelter of these latitudes? Far better the heavy seas around the rugged coast of Newfoundland. You will cool off up there, sailor, and that of itself should be a destination worthy of the voyage.

But after this cheery speech, the captain again lapsed into silence. And your will, he began at last.

That was not what McQuade had expected. He didn't want to hear anything about his will.

I would not have dared to bring up the subject, the captain explained, except that you kept mentioning, in your delirium, your desire to bequeath something of value to Sally Sunstrum. How you wanted to look after your darling Sally!

Sally? echoed McQuade. You would remind me of her? My mother implied I would die if I didn't marry Sally. But I have no reason to leave anything to Sally. What would I leave her? What do I have to leave?

The three rings? the captain suggested.

McQuade grew alarmed. I have no rings, he protested. Those rings have nothing to do with Sally. How do you know about those rings? Believe me, I have nothing to leave Sally but my love. And he beat his bandaged hand against the mattress of his bunk.

Forgive me for bringing up her name, the captain said. But I assure you, your dreams were full of Sally.

What good would it do to leave anything to Sally, love or rings? McQuade asked himself. Sally was already dead. She had been rescued by Fortune, only to die in the arms of Sanderson. Somehow he had pictured the scene so clearly. Up to a point, that is. Thereafter, events were murky. And only moments later, Sanderson had taken his own life. And Gabriella dead in the streets, shot down by who knew what side or for what reason. And Fortune snuffed out before the firing squad; even now McQuade could make himself hear the crack of the volley and the bullets tear into the crumble that had become the wall.

Later, the captain was replaced in the cabin by de Groot and Pendleton. Paying our respects, said Pendleton, finding him awake.

McQuade took their hands. At least you were able to make good your escape, he said. When Sanderson found the Seafarers deserted, I feared for the worst. But I hadn't known you planned to join us on the *Evergreen*?

Any ship in a storm, de Groot explained.

I must tell you that none of our friends made it, McQuade said.

Strange that you should know that, was Pendleton's opinion.

Not so strange, McQuade answered, when none of them are here.

He means that you should know with such certainty the reasons for their absence, de Groot said, which to your way of thinking is best explained by their being dead. Doesn't it strike you as extraordinary that you would be familiar with the very circumstances of their deaths? How do you come by such knowledge? How were you there? Or are we to conclude that you possess psychic powers that enable you to witness, long distance, such unhappy events as they occur?

I will take it a step further, Pendleton declared. It is as if you were yourself the author of these disasters.

God knows I am guilty of many sins, McQuade protested. But you go too far in such an accusation.

Oh, your comrades didn't really die, de Groot explained. Or, I should say, they died, but not really. Nor is it as if they can't be resurrected, having failed to die properly in the first place.

Their deaths were real enough, McQuade said, shuddering.

But what if all this mayhem is only the work of your feverish imagination rattling about the inner landscapes of your brain? Pendleton suggested.

If that is the case, your friends could still be alive, de Groot explained. With your permission, I will bring the notion home to you in the most dramatic fashion. Mitzi, the daughter of the ambassador, is aboard this ship. No, her body hasn't been recovered from the sea. She was picked out of the water alive by the crew of a foreign freighter, who placed her aboard the *Evergreen.* A bullet nicked her shoulder and she swallowed some seawater, but otherwise she is no worse than if she had gone for a swim. We have just come from seeing her.

It is unclear, Pendleton added, whether or not she sends you her best.

And what of Gabriella? McQuade wondered. I suppose you will tell me she isn't dead when I know for a fact that Fortune saw her body in the street.

No, he thought he might have seen it, de Groot

corrected. But he did not verify the corpse as hers. She escaped Smoke Street as she said she would. She was much too crafty and slippery to have been caught.

And I suppose Fortune wasn't executed, McQuade said.

Of course he wasn't. He bribed the sentry with one of the three rings—he had kept two back, having needed only one to ransom Sally—and escaped in the confusion of the rebel attack upon the old military academy. Nor was Sanderson a suicide. He couldn't bring himself to take the poison. Nor to administer it to Sally. Instead, he gathered her in his arms and rushed out into the street, where he managed to flag down the last army truck to escape the rebel advance into the area.

Which means that Sally is alive after all! McQuade exclaimed.

Exactly, de Groot said. Rejoice in the good news! This is the message we have come to deliver, if you will let us. Sally lives!

However, this means, of course, that you must die, Pendleton said.

What an extraordinary thing to say, McQuade thought. As if one followed the other in some illogical cause and effect. Pendleton's contention was so easy to refute. The evidence to the contrary was no less than himself. His corporeal self. The feel of his flesh, the sound of his voice, the sightfulness of his eyes. Why should I die? he protested.

Why shouldn't you, when you are very nearly dead already? was Pendleton's rejoinder.

Obviously I am not dead, McQuade argued. Nor am I dying. Even if I was in a bad way, I have recovered. How else could I be here with you in this cabin, speaking, listening, thinking, resting up for the remainder, kicking up a fuss?

Above all, thinking, de Groot commented.

Still, he has raised a point that demands an answer, Pendleton admitted.

One must fight to stay alive, McQuade thought. One must not give up without a struggle.

Would you believe me if I told you, de Groot said, that after seeing both yourself and Mitzi, it is my opinion that it is not she who is moribund, but you, McQuade?

Do I look as though I am at death's door? McQuade demanded.

Embarrassed, de Groot appealed to his friend for the help that was not forthcoming. Finally he said, You do not look well.

There is the matter of your morbid sweat, Pendleton observed.

Who calls it morbid? McQuade objected. What do you expect in such a torrid climate? Look at the way you sweat yourselves. Believe me, you would sweat like me if you had experienced my sorrows and dangers.

Still, McQuade had to admit, it was the hollowest of victories, living through his story as he had. Turning out to be a survivor when so many whom he hoped to save had perished.

Understand me, de Groot said. If Mitzi is dead, it was you who killed her. You did her in because of your selfish instinct for survival and didn't give her death a second thought.

A new line of defense occurred to McQuade. How do you know so much better than I the fate of my friends? he asked. Were you there? Do you have psychic powers? He had thrown back the very questions de Groot had asked him earlier.

In time, all things will be made known to you, was de Groot's answer.

As if he didn't already know them, Pendleton said.

In the meantime, the captain has sent for your mother and father, de Groot said.

His mother and father stood above McQuade while de Groot and Pendleton retreated to the background. Father wore his black tie and white dinner jacket, double-breasted; Mother wore her nurse's unform.

Give up the farm, his father said.

Marry the girl, said his mother.

What are you doing here? said McQuade, astounded. How is it that you are in the present time and aboard my ship? You belong to an earlier time and a different place. A midwestern setting, somewhere. True, I saw you earlier, but those scenes were so obviously a vision or hallucination, seen by no one but myself. And yet, here you are, mingling with real people, in the real world. How is such a confusion possible?

They are merely the living proof of what we have been telling you, de Groot explained. For what was then is now, and what was there is here. What was lived was dreamed. And all vice versa. All times are one time, and always have been, and, at the same time, have been no time at all. A revolving door opens onto all the rooms, and through it, all the times are free to come and go. You see, there was only an illusion of time passing in the many scenes and episodes that came before. The only time that truly passed was the time you took to dream it up. And this occurred during the time of the black earth and orange sky. A frozen time. A most singular time. Deadly, too. Without any need of clocks and calendars.

The ambassador and the naval attaché joined the others in the cabin. They were escorted by the captain and the chief engineer in their immaculate drill whites.

Why not let my daughter live? the ambassador implored. I have come to take her ashore. It is safe to do so at this hour. A truce has been declared between the warring factions, and all sides have declared the capital an open city. There is even talk of a general amnesty.

That explains the eerie silence of the cannon, the captain said.

Come, do as the ambassador asks, only you can change the course of destiny, his father said.

Or appear to, Pendleton corrected.

But according to your crazy logic, McQuade complained, asking me to let Mitzi live is the same as asking me to die.

Still, you reach the same conclusion no matter which way you decide, his father said.

He used to be a little scholar, his mother said. He was liked well enough by his teachers, beloved of his classmates. Oftentimes he was closer to the bottom of his class than to the top. He was never a quick learner. You would think a basic course in physics would have told him the way matters stood these days. But I must tell you that when he did reach a conclusion of sorts, he held onto it tenaciously. He was not about to give it up without a fight. A little bulldog, we called him.

More like a rat terrier, his father said.

I should have said he was like a faithful Newfoundland, Captain Lundholm said. To save a drowning shipmate he would have thrown his small self into the stormy seas.

His father said, Can't you see how you are upsetting the balance of nature by continuing to hang around?

If he is allowed to get away with this, said the naval attaché, we might as well walk on our heads and think with our feet. The next you know, the sky will be raining roses and cellars will change places with attics.

That is true, the captain said. What if I tried to sail my ship over sand? Or used a rudder for a sail?

Exactly, said the attaché. There is a certain way to act, and all actions must be performed in those certain ways, or they do not become those actions, and nothing makes any sense.

In the great law-abiding scheme of the universe,

his father said, not so much as a single hair on a lemur was ever out of place until you, McQuade, made your move.

De Groot put it this way. Why can't you accept the consequences of being a man? Why wish the longevity of an elephant, a whale, a tortoise, a parrot, when with just a pinch of sacrifice and resolution you could rise above those beasts? Not that they haven't been known to look out for one another, he added.

You do have a choice, his father said. The resolutions of the heart, unlike those of the flesh, are never mandatory.

Or so we like to think, was Pendleton's opinion.

Friends! McQuade called out, his eyes wide, his mouth gaping as his head shot up from the pillow while the rest of him flattened out upon the bunk, I am dying!

No sooner had he spoken than Mitzi herself appeared before him, right up front, too, let through by the others. Her eyes were wide and discriminating, and she smiled at him, showing the perfection of her teeth. Undeniably, she was in the glow of health. For the benefit of those who had not been present, the naval attaché recounted the miracle of her recovery—her sudden second recovery. For although she had been rescued once already, plucked from the water into which she had been tossed, she had suffered a relapse once McQuade had come aboard and insisted no such rescue had taken place after all. But once Mc-

Quade had come to his senses and faced up to the awful truth, she had opened her eyes, caught her first breath and sighed, while those around her had observed the limpness leave her limbs. They had stood her up carefully, ready to catch her if she swooned. She swayed, leaned way backward with the back of her hand pressed against her forehead, but was quick to right herself. Then she took the first step. Bravo! her father shouted, clapping, beside himself with joy. The naval attaché, in his happiness, hugged and kissed her.

Of course, you know what this means, de Groot said, regarding the consequences of your actions.

McQuade nodded.

You have cheated the death squads, Pendleton said, admiringly. That is what you have done.

Soon, Sanderson and Sally were among the crowd around his bunk. So was Fortune. And Gabriella. McQuade caught sight of their faces behind the others. Newcomers were present, too, but too far back for him to see distinctly.

No one can hurt you now, his mother said.

They can't arrest you either, his father added. I am thinking, naturally, of the theft of those rings.

The naval attaché said, I suppose those rings are gone for good. You wouldn't want to tell us what you did with them, McQuade, before you go?

Mitzi said, I wouldn't mind wearing them again. I loved the way they sparkled in the light. Look how ugly my hands have become without them. Just wrinkled skin, nails and bone.

Why, those are beautiful hands, the naval attaché

said, kissing them. Why do you talk so? And those are beautiful arms attached to your hands, and demarcated by beautiful wrists and elbows.

Of course they are, her father said. And you are a magnificent young woman from head to toe.

I don't believe you, she said. Either of you. You are both saying that to make up for the rings.

There, there, said the ambassador, we will get you another ring.

Three rings, promised the naval attaché.

But not the same rings, she complained. Not like before. When I was a little girl I would tell myself I would never die so long as I wore my prettiest rings.

And someone took them knowing that, you say, the ambassador said.

Oh, Daddy, I don't know what to think! she wailed.

The ambassador addressed himself to McQuade. We know you persuaded Sanderson to steal them for you, and that you received them as stolen goods. But we forgive you. For that and other crimes and misdemeanors. We don't want you to leave us guilty.

McQuade could only catch an occasional flutter of hands above his face, and that distorted as though separated from him by thick, imperfect glass. The voices faded in and out of his hearing. Don't leave me, friends, he cried.

We only leave when you leave, his father said.

It is not so much that we are leaving you, his mother said, as it is you who is leaving us.

McQuade began to catch the drift of what they

said. Mother, he asked, would you say my face will be in my sister's sons?

She said, You have no sister.

No sister, McQuade repeated. And I suppose no brother.

No brother, McQuade, she said.

McQuade overheard the naval attaché saying, I should think if he did have sisters and brothers and they did have sons that those fellows would have their own faces!

There was much laughter all around at his remark. Laughter that grew fainter. And farther away.

Wait, McQuade said. I can stay if you don't go.

So long, old sailor, Captain Lundholm said. We must take her out of this steaming port.

Believe me, McQuade said, reaching out to seize his wrist and hold him if he could, I would be happy to go with you—nothing would suit me better! But I can't move much anymore. I don't like to leave you shorthanded on such short notice. I hope you can find another hand.

The captain gently removed his hand. He turned to McQuade's parents and said, So like your son to trouble about the other fellow even at a time when no man in his right mind would envy him his fate.

We will give him a funeral fit for a deckhand, the chief engineer said. We will have a thousand kazoos and penny whistles. Half a thousand Jew's harps. A hundred tambourines. About the same amount of washboards. But two thousand combs with paper. And all playing, "Asleep in the Deep." And for a farewell salute, a child with a tackhammer and a roll of caps, busy on the sidewalk.

Voices murmured assent in the crowd. As McQuade watched, the naval attaché attached himself to Mitzi; Sanderson put his arm around Sally and drew her to him; Fortune took the hand of Gabriella.

McQuade's mother said, He has been killing time all his life.

An eye for an eye, the captain muttered.

The ambassador frowned and pointed at McQuade with his arm outstretched. Therefore, he said, pronouncing sentence, let time kill him!

After such a scene, McQuade had no reason to believe he would see any more of this world, but then there were de Groot and Pendleton alone with him in the cabin. De Groot still wearing the rumpled safari suit and using that cheap Hong Kong fan and his large handkerchief to cool his sweaty face. He sat in a chair he had moved up close to the bunk. Pendleton stood behind him, peering over his shoulder.

Why? McQuade said.

Are you a musician, McQuade? de Groot asked. Ever play the piano?

McQuade shook his head.

Too bad, he said. I might have said your note was needed for the harmony, and you would have known what I meant.

Is it that you can't sail without a full complement of crew? McQuade suggested.

You sail alone, Pendleton explained. And you don't sail so much as sink.

De Groot said, It is my opinion that you found it difficult to die alone. That is the best explanation for your having created us. We were needed to keep you company. Also to test you—but I will come to that. What, didn't know you had created us? We were only performing to the best of our abilities the parts you had given us to play. We were never more than the refractions of that natural world out there that time and space and circumstances determined you would dream up at the end. We were all, including you yourself, McQuade, inside your head. All of us, self-contained. So was everything else you authored. The then and now. The here and there. The action and contemplation. There was only an illusion of space. Also of time. This then, McQuade, was the final vision. Plot and characters, they were nothing but the sum of you. Or what is left of you.

What galaxies are to be found inside the human mind, Pendleton said respectfully. Even in one so young.

If he is that young, de Groot said.

Exactly, Pendleton said. For McQuade was as much your creation as the rest of us. You may not be a sailor at all, but a landlubber who sickens with *mal de mer* at the sight of a duck pond. And you need not be a youngster either, you could be an old codger—you might even be a woman! There is no way we will ever know. And your name probably isn't McQuade either. It could be Honeycutt, or Carruthers. Or Charlie de Sousa. It could even be Elmer Charade.

If you found it difficult to die alone, de Groot said, you found it just as difficult to die without a reason. So you imagined and committed a human sacrifice. Your own. A selfless act which explains your death and lends it dignity. A death which, occurring as it must in the world outside your consciousness, would have otherwise been wasted and inconsequential. So you suffered the consequences. That is my theory, anyway. Naturally, you wanted to live—it was hard getting past that desire—but you also wanted love, and that meant you were willing to sacrifice yourself for others. Such a tenderness, such a storehouse of love you had pent up within you. A love you imagined, to suit the circumstances, as romantic, desperate, doomed. You effected the rescue of Sally, but only up to a point, for you denied her when it became obvious that your own life was at risk. Much in the same manner, you betrayed your other friends. You sent Fortune in search of Gabriella, knowing that along the way the soldiers lay in wait. Nor would you let the beleaguered Sanderson escape Smoke Street, where you had shut him up with Sally. Poor devil, despite his several desperate attempts to escape, he never had a chance. You had stacked the deck against him. However, it might be said in your defense that, like the ancients who took their most prized possessions with them to the grave under the illusion that they would enjoy them in the world to come, you desired only to take your friends into what you hoped would be the afterlife. But you could never bring yourself to actually see them dead; you could not go all the way in completing their destruction. And in this reluctance was the foreshadowing of the change of heart that was to come. When the guilt and moral implications of your plan to do away with them became intolerable, you relented and delivered yourself into the hands of death, where you belonged, so that Mitzi, the daughter of the ambassador, might live. After such a breakthrough, other resurrections followed.

It is you who are the time machine, said Pendleton. The place does not exist that you cannot visit. There is no time you can't hear ticking. Nothing you cannot say or do.

For the first time McQuade realized that this man was a puppet in his hands and that he had made him say these words. Now that he was resolved to accept the consequences and had had the situation explained to him, why couldn't he do with this cast of characters as he liked? Why not take them with him after all? Where else could they go if not with him? In what other landscape and time frame could they possibly exist?

This opened up a final possibility.

A powerful explosion rocked the ship. It was all McQuade could do to keep from tumbling out of his bunk.

We have hit a mine! a sailor shouted.

We have been torpedoed! said another.

All about them, the hiss of steam, the smell of smoke, a heavy bell clanging, a siren.

What an irony, Pendleton said, that this should happen after a truce has been declared.

All hands and passengers were out on deck. McQuade himself was carried out on a stretcher. The ship was listing badly to starboard. The smoke drifted across the deck like fog.

De Groot had his hat on his head and his briefcase in hand, ready to go. He said, I suppose if you could, Captain, you would order us all into the lifeboats.

But the captain said, Wait a minute. I recognize you. Didn't we meet once in Kuala Lumpur? Something to do with a cargo of copra. Or were you dealing in rhinoceros' horns?

These remarks caught the attention of the ambassador, who seemed to be aware of de Groot for the first time. And didn't I know you in Tangier? he said, when I was chargé d'affaires in the mission there? A stolen passport ring, wasn't that what you had your hands in? Only it was a Mr. Greenfield then. Where do you come by the name of de Groot?

Well, well, you have the advantage, gentlemen, de Groot admitted. As they say, the jig is up.

Pendleton shook his head. So much death and destruction, he muttered. Boats torpedoed in the harbor for no reason. And that awful revolution in the streets. Store windows smashed, pawnshops looted, terrible things.

I wish I could escape it all, every bit of it, McQuade said. I wish with all my soul I could take a night plane to Paris.

I wouldn't mind throwing it all up, McQuade's father said. The city, the civilization, the social scale, all those late hours in the supper club, playing for drunks, and the sentry duty in the cold gusts at the revolving door. I wouldn't mind retiring to your little island, Mr. Pendleton, off the coast of Maine. I would be willing to begin anew if that were possible. I would gather mussels to start with. I would break my back, forking up those clams.

I have my memories of that island, Pendleton said. And of the sea life in its many forms that was found along those shores. That cannot be taken from me.

McQuade's mother gave him a final check. He is leaving, she said, and taking us with him.

He wants to have me after all, Mitzi said. Even though he sacrificed himself that I may live. I ask you, is that fair of him?

He wants me, too, said Sally. Now that I have become serious about another man. And she gazed up at Sanderson, who stood beside her on the deck.

Fortune and Gabriella had nothing to say to each other, or to anyone else. They simply embraced and kissed.

At long last he has done as he was told, his mother said.

We are all pounding on the bars of his cranium, de Groot said. Hoping to escape.

We never did get out of his head, said the naval attaché, regardless of much illusory evidence to the contrary.

It's like finding yourself down in the engine room after your ship has struck a reef, said the chief engineer, with the seawater pouring in through the plates and the neighboring compartments closing their portals against your escape.

I don't want to die, Sally said.

Me neither, said Sanderson.

Courage, comrades, said the captain.

We are sinking, said the chief.

Which said it best for all of them.

McQuade returned briefly to the embassy. Through the corner of his filmy eye he caught sight of de Groot and the ambassador walking arm in arm to the window, where the latter pulled back the drapes.

If you were in any condition to look out this window, McQuade, the ambassador remarked, you would observe how, at long last, the sun is going up or down.

And, if you had binoculars, said de Groot, you would make out how that freighter in the harbor is raising anchor in preparation for her departure from the port.

Notice how the earth is turning green again, pointed out the ambassador. And, above it, how the sky is turning blue.

But the last sight McQuade saw on this earth was the picnic. His eyes were open, too. They were fixed upon this picnic. He saw how he wasn't a member of its party. He had no idea where he could have gone off to.

The coastline south of the capital is a low-lying jungle, but to the north the mountains meet the sea, with the land arid along the heights. Here, during the truce that continues to hold in the city and countryside, the picnic is taking place. Blankets have been spread on a patch of grass where only minutes earlier goats grazed. For the moment, napkins and tablecloths have been draped on a nearby clump of bushes. Several wicker baskets are open on the blankets. So are two bottles of white wine. The three highly polished automobiles that lumbered up the wagon path of whitish sand that winds upward through the grass are parked around the blankets, as though to light them with their headlights should that prove necessary. Two are sports models; the other is a limousine. The air is misty, but quickly clearing, and suggests a time of morning that is not long after sunrise. Since most of the picnickers are in evening dress, it seems reasonable to assume that they are the survivors of some all-night gala affair who have gone on a whim for a picnic breakfast at the seaside. There is both a rosiness and a pallor to their faces, as though the open air is contending with the dissipation of last night. The men are speaking softly in graceful sallies of wit and flattery, and the women can be heard laughing in response.

A young man in the uniform of a navel cadet holds out a drumstick to a handsome blonde girl who, also on her knees, plays the begging puppy and takes it in her mouth. He has made her lips and chin so greasy with his chicken. A married couple in their mid-thirties sit side by side on folding chairs. He looks like a passenger on an ocean voyage with his little cap, tartan blanket, travel book, Czar Nicholas beard. His handsome wife serves them from a large silver tray, egg-salad sandwiches cut into triangles from which the crusts have been sliced. An engaged couple sits on a blanket, back to back, like bookends. She nibbles on a carrot stick; he drinks a glass of wine. The cadet who has been watching them, suddenly laughs. Simultaneously, each has looked over a shoulder, so that they confront each other face to face. She exchanges her carrot for his wine as they wink and kiss. It is this that has amused the cadet. The older man with the beard has risen and, now that the mist has lifted, is searching the sea with his binoculars.

On the blue water of the sunlit bay a great white freighter is passing between the green headlands of the river mouth, making for the open sea beyond. It gives a wide berth to the grand cruiser scuttled earlier in the week, some of whose damaged superstructure shows above the water. A new flag is observed going up over the old Spanish fort on the island.

There is no sound to the freighter's sailing from this distance. Nor can it be seen to move. Even so, it grows smaller and more distant. Already it seems to have entered a different zone of reference entirely. As though it sails on another ocean. Light-years away.

The binoculars are replaced by a telescope in the hands of the viewer, and a pilot is made out leaving the ship in a launch and waving good-bye to those in the wheelhouse.

Bon voyage, McQuade!